THE PHYSICIAN'S GUN

INSPIRED BY TRUE EVENTS

JOHN EVAN HARRIS

ROIALL EMERALD PUBLISHING

Henry Appleton
Gun for hire, adventurer,
gold prospector, trapper, lawmaker.
Hero of the West.

CONTENTS

AUTHOR'S NOTE

It is my hope that reading *The Physician's Gun* will inspire young readers to learn more about the early days of European settlement in New Zealand – not just about the notorious Burgess gang, about whom there have been several books written and many articles – but about what life was like for the settlers, and for Māori. There are many books, websites and locations to explore. A list of some of them appears at the end of this book, along with historical photographs of Burgess and Nelson at the time.

ONE
DEAD ENOUGH

Henry Appleton jumped to his feet and grabbed the doctor's bag.

He swung it hard, knocking the gun out of Kelly's hands, and charged away like a hunted animal. *Run, run!*

A dark shape burst from the forest, waving a rusty shovel in the air.

"Come back, you little toad!" Sullivan roared.

Not on your life! Henry kept running.

"Get him!" Sullivan yelled.

Kelly leapt to his feet and followed with the physician's gun.

Henry ran hell for leather, arms flailing, doctor's bag swinging. *I'm faster! They won't catch me.*

Then, abruptly, he stopped.

He was at the top of a steep ravine. Far below was a shallow creek full of rocks.

I'm trapped! What can I do?

Behind him, Sullivan drew his pistol.

I'm going to die like a dog! Shaking, Henry raised the doctor's bag in front of his chest and closed his eyes.

Sullivan squeezed the trigger and *crack*! The bullet whistled though the air and smacked into the doctor's bag. The bag absorbed the impact of the bullet, but it threw Henry off balance. He slipped backwards over the edge and tumbled down the bank, smashing through bushes, still clutching the bag.

CRACK! The bullet whistled though the air and smacked into the doctor's bag.

Sullivan and Kelly, panting from their chase, appeared at the top of the ravine and watched Henry fall.

He crashed into the creek and lay there, dazed. Through blurry eyes he saw a thin trail of his blood snake into the water.

"He's dead," said Kelly.

"Maybe. Maybe not," said Sullivan. "Git down there an' finish him awf. An' get the bag."

Sullivan ran back to join the gang, and Kelly squinted at Henry in the creek.

"He looks dead enough," he muttered.

Henry didn't move a muscle. *Please don't come down here and check on me!*

"Hey!" Kelly shouted.

Play dead! Henry turned his face away but kept his eyes wide open as he listened to Kelly. Rama's scarf, gripped in his hand, trailed in the current of the stream.

"Hey, you!" Kelly called. He picked up a rock the size of a man's fist and took aim.

The rock spun through the air and smacked into Henry's leg with a dull *thunk*.

Henry's face screwed up. *Aaaaaagh!!!* He screamed silently as pain shot through his leg. But still he didn't move.

Kelly looked down on Henry's body, lying crumpled in the stream.

Henry felt the ache seep through his body. He screwed up his face as a jumble of images and thoughts cascaded through his head. Sullivan's hands around his throat. His father's headstone: *Bring justice to the fatherless*. The physician's gun.

His longing to have a gun of his own.

My leg hurts so badly. God help me!

I'm going to die and no one will ever find me and—

I'm not even sixteen.

Henry Appleton, lying in a nameless creek somewhere in the dark hills above his home, waited to die.

TWO
HIS FATHER'S RIFLE

Henry's troubles had begun the day the physician arrived. Just a week previously.

It was June 6, 1866. Henry stood in the shadow of the back door. Behind the cottage, enclosed by a rickety fence, was a well-hoed garden with neat rows of potatoes, carrots, and spinach. Further back, separated by another fence, was their cow, Alberta, and several hens wandering free.

They had named it Bluebell Cottage. It was a sturdy settlers' cottage, purchased by his father William Appleton soon after they had arrived from England with boxes crammed with everything from shoes to kitchen chairs.

The name was Henry's mother's idea: Victoria hoped soon to see delicate English bluebells flourishing in their front yard. But so far, none had appeared.

It had been only six months since the worst day of Henry's short life: his father's death. William Appleton had been down at Canvas Town, one of thousands of desperate men searching for gold, when he collapsed. Heart attack, they said.

They named it Bluebell Cottage: Henry's mother hoped soon to
see delicate English bluebells flourishing in their front yard.

Henry knew his father was a good man, of course; a
man of honour. But not a strong man. He'd only gone to the
goldfields because the family was short of money.

When news of William Appleton's death reached
Nelson, young Henry and his mother were in the garden,
tending the vegetables to earn enough money to survive
another winter.

Victoria had already sold her pearl necklace to pay for
flour. And soon the bank would be knocking on the door,

demanding the Appletons catch up with their mortgage payments.

And then suddenly William Appleton was gone, and Henry and his mother were alone.

At fifteen, Henry was very much a man in the eyes of the town. Big and strong enough to dig the garden, mend the fences, ride the horse.

But although he didn't like to admit it, he was in many ways still a boy, and he knew his mother was perhaps a bit soft on him.

Henry watched his mother digging fiercely.

She was in her late thirties, thin and muscular. She wore threadbare trousers from his father's wardrobe, rolled up and hitched with a piece of cord; and the shirt was Henry's, knotted at the waist, with a black armband.

It had been a long time since his mother had worn a pretty dress, back in London. Sometimes she talked to Henry about those times: days of chamber music and dances and Sunday strolls in Hyde Park.

Henry could just remember his mother taking him as a young boy to join the crowds outside Kensington Palace, cheering as the Queen of England set out in her carriage.

His mother had the same Christian name as Her Majesty, who right now was probably sleeping in a four-poster bed with gold adornments. Queen Victoria – so well-fed, they said, that one rude doctor commented she was "more like a barrel than anything else".

And here on the other side of the globe was his mother, Victoria Appleton, widowed, poor and thin, stomping around in the mud under a blazing sun.

How does she keep going?

Like his mother, Henry was lean and hardened from their hand-to-mouth existence. He knew he should be working alongside her. Instead, he quietly retrieved his father's rifle from under his mother's bed and went to his small bedroom at the front of the cottage.

He leaned out the window, aiming the weapon at imaginary villains in the forest. "Pow! Pow!"

The rifle was an Enfield cavalry carbine: heavy, and not easy to handle, but Henry knew it was deadly accurate at long distances. He stroked the well-oiled wooden stock and dreamed of the day he would feel the punch of the rifle's recoil as he dispatched another Indian Brave.

"Henry!"

He didn't register his mother's call, and continued to gaze out the window. From here, he had a clear view of the front yard and the forest beyond.

He fiddled with the lucky rabbit's foot attached to the rifle. Strange that his father, a God-fearing man who read the Bible every morning, should believe a trinket would bring him luck. *And it didn't.* But now that his father had gone, little things like a rabbit's foot brought comfort.

"Henry!"

This time, Henry jumped. "Coming!"

Henry darted into his mother's room, returned the rifle to its baize-lined strongbox, and pushed it back under her bed. He was careful not to disturb his father's polished boots, parked neatly at the end of the bed.

A thought flashed through Henry's mind: *Father will never wear these again.*

The soles of his own boots were so thin he could feel the pebbles he stepped on. But he knew his father's boots would fit him; he had tried them on when his mother was gardening.

Several times.

THREE
THE DIME NOVEL

Henry emerged from the cottage.

"Look," said his mother.

Standing in the adjoining field, with a blanket around his stooped shoulders, was an elderly Māori man with a heavily tattooed face.

Henry had seen men like this in town. "Natives", they were called by those locals who didn't care for them much. He'd heard some people call them "rebels", too. And "savages".

The scars that adorned the old man's face intrigued Henry, and he winced when he thought how painful it must be to have a tattoo chiselled into your flesh.

The old man shuffled to a makeshift shelter made of mānuka branches, thatched with ferns to keep off the sun. A boy about Henry's age helped him. He was Māori too, but too young to be tattooed.

The boy gave a cheery wave, and Henry waved back. "Why are they here?" he asked.

"It's their land."

Their land? In past decades, it had been Māori tribes who had fought over land, but these days the arguments were between Māori people and the Europeans.

Their land? Henry knew that years before he and his parents had arrived in New Zealand, there had been a violent encounter at Wairau, just down the coast. Twenty-two white people and four Māori had been killed.

Many Europeans called it a massacre and blamed the Māori, but the Governor had investigated it and declared that it was the white people, armed with rifles and swords, who were to blame.

Some white people around these parts were still fearful of Māori people, even though the white settlers now outnumbered them.

Henry had tried to find out more, but the moment he mentioned the word "Wairau", people clammed up. Even more than twenty years later, what had happened that day was still raw.

Henry watched the old Māori man and his young companion make themselves at home on the land across the fence. "I thought the land belonged to Mister Chadwick," he said.

"Mister Chadwick thinks it does."

His mother almost spat the name. No one liked Mister Chadwick, the bank manager, but they were polite to his face because he seemed to own half of everything around here. Including Bluebell Cottage.

An enormous pig appeared at their fence line, and snuffled in the soil.

"Shoo!" Henry hurled a clod of dirt and the animal

lumbered away. His mother grabbed a sagging fence post and pushed it upright.

"Chadwick's pigs are going to get through again," she said.

Henry helped her with the fence post, absent-minded.

"Henry?"

"Yes?"

"You promised to fix the fence."

"Sorry, Mother. I will."

His mother slopped a bucket of water into a trough for Alberta, picked a bunch of wildflowers, and went inside. Henry abandoned the fence post and followed her.

He slipped into his bedroom and slumped on his bed. He heard his mother put water in a pot on the hearth, and from under his mattress he pulled out a dime novel.

The American trapper on the cover had shoulder-length hair and a drooping moustache. Wild Bill Hickok, Indian Slayer, stood in an heroic pose, dressed in animal furs and holding a long rifle.

If only I lived in the Wild West, Henry dreamed. *With a gun of my own.*

Under his breath, he sang his favourite ditty: "A man needs a gun to be someone…"

The door swung open and his mother marched in.

"Mother! This is my room!"

She grabbed the novel. "Where did you get this?" She studied the cover. "Wild Bill Hickok? 'Indian Slayer'?" She shook her head. "This is not a man to be admired, Henry."

"He's a lawman," Henry shot back.

"And a killer, by the looks. Indians are people, Henry, not wild animals."

"It's a true story," Henry muttered.

"I'll warrant most of it is not true," his mother retorted. She looked closely at the cover. "Written by Johnny Slick. 'Johnny Slick'? What kind of name is that?"

"He's my favourite writer!"

"You've read more of his rubbish?"

"*Shootout at Dead Man's Creek.*"

"What a waste of your pocket money."

"At least he's not stuffy like Charles Dickens," Henry snapped.

"Dickens has something to say," said his mother.

"So does Johnny Slick."

"You enjoyed *A Christmas Carol*."

"It was soppy."

"And what about *A Tale of Two Cities*? We loved reading that."

"I know," Henry admitted. " 'It was the best of times, it was the worst of times.' "

"Yes," said his mother. "The worst of times."

She tossed the dime novel on his bed, dislodging a small photograph mounted on a piece of card. She picked it up.

"A *carte de visite*?" She had received them from time to time, from family back in England. They were usually photographs of sorely missed friends or a familiar London street scene.

This one showed a man with intense eyes and a horse-shoe moustache. His long hair was pinned under a small cloth forage cap, worn at a jaunty angle. He stood in a proud pose with a large sword at his side.

"And who is this?"

"Von Tempsky," Henry mumbled.

"Another man with a strange name."

"He's a New Zealand soldier," Henry shot back. "The Forest Rangers."

"Strange little hat he's wearing," said his mother. "And expensive boots." She dropped the card on Henry's bed and left the room.

Henry looked at the photo of Major Gustavus von Tempsky and the sketch of Wild Bill Hickok. *What adventurers!* They both used the Colt .36, he had found out.

He called after his mother: "Wild Bill's father died when he was the same age as me." He knew that would sting.

He watched as Victoria Appleton looked over at the wall where a framed studio portrait of her husband had pride of place. His fob watch hung next to it, still ticking. She pulled her apron tight and turned to the stove.

Henry emerged from his room and perched on the solid wooden chest that had carried their clothes from England. He remembered his father hauling it up from the port on a sled, along the muddy tracks through the hills.

"Father would've let me use his rifle."

His mother sighed. "Probably, yes. But he was a dreamer."

Henry gripped the familiar iron trim of the sea chest. "He knew I wanted to be a writer."

"Henry," she said, "we've been over this before. You've got the brains to be a lawyer or a doctor. Or a teacher, like your father."

"I'd rather be a writer."

"Your world is too full of make-believe."

"Well, why can't I have Father's rifle?"

His mother gave the same answer she'd given so many times before. "A gun does not make you a man, Henry."

Usually, this argument would go on for a few more minutes. But not today. Through the front door, Henry had seen something in the woods.

"Mother – look!"

In the dark shadow of the trees, maybe fifty yards away, was a man on horseback.

He sat straight-backed in the saddle, like a cavalry officer, dressed in black. His right hand supported the muzzle of a rifle that rested in a leather bucket attached to the horse's flank.

And tied to the saddle was a leather doctor's bag.

But it was the stranger's hat that drew Henry's attention. It was a top hat, the kind worn by wealthy gentlemen in town, and it seemed out of place here in the mountains.

A word came to mind; a word his mother had recently taught him. It was "incongruous".

"How long has he been there?" whispered his mother. She stepped out, with Henry close behind.

The horse and rider began moving towards them. Slowly.

Under his top hat, the visitor's face was pale and his piercing eyes had the appearance of someone who had not slept well for a long time.

Henry drew back. "Who is he?" he whispered. His mother put a reassuring hand on his arm.

There was a movement under the trees, and they realised the stranger was not alone. Another horse and rider appeared from the shadows behind him, leading a scrawny packhorse.

Henry and his mother waited.

In the dark shadow of the trees was a man on horseback. His right hand supported the muzzle of a rifle.

FOUR

VISITORS

THE STRANGER STOPPED HIS HORSE A FEW YARDS FROM HENRY and his mother, and tipped his hat.

"Welcome," said Victoria Appleton.

The stranger slipped from his saddle with practised ease, and bowed. "Morning, Ma'am."

His clipped voice was that of an English gentleman. *But why does he hold his throat when he talks?*

Henry ventured closer to study the visitor – or more particularly, his rifle. Even from the little he could see of it, he guessed it was a Calisher and Terry carbine, shorter and easier to load than his father's Enfield.

"Allow me to introduce myself. The name is Smith. Doctor Smith."

Henry frowned, and studied the embossed words on the visitor's bag: Z. Smith.

What does Z stand for? Is he really a doctor?

Henry saw his mother smile and brush the dirt from her hands.

"And this…" Z. Smith turned to his young companion,

who was examining the packhorse's hoof. "This is Rama, my guide. And translator."

Rama nodded, but kept his face hidden under the generous brim of his hat. Before Henry could take a closer look, Rama moved out of sight behind the packhorse. *Strange,* thought Henry. *They're both strange.*

Henry's mother curtsied. He hadn't seen her do that in a long time. "Victoria Appleton. Pleased to make your acquaintance."

The doctor snapped the heels of his boots together and offered another bow.

"And my son, Henry."

Smith nodded in Henry's direction but continued to address his mother. "We've travelled some distance. Might we water our horses?"

"Certainly," Henry's mother answered. Henry's gaze had returned to the visitor's rifle. *I'd really like a closer look.*

"Henry?"

Henry knew his mother was keen for conversation. Very few travellers passed this way, and none as well-spoken as Z. Smith.

With a sigh, he picked up a bucket and walked off.

Smith pointed at the packhorse's ankle. "She needs rest."

"You are from London?" asked Henry's mother.

"Indeed," he replied.

Henry returned and gave Rama a bucket of water.

"Kia ora," the young man replied.

Henry was unsure how to respond. He hadn't spoken to a Māori person his own age before.

"Hello," he ventured. "Umm … me Henry."

Rama grinned. "Me Rama," he said in a gentle voice, then laughed. "I too speak the Queen's English."

"Oh – sorry," Henry blustered. "I thought…"

But Rama was gone, leading the packhorse to the door of the barn.

Smith indicated Henry's horse, Duke. It was his pride and joy: a reward from the bank when a much younger Henry had helped to catch a bank robber.

"Is your horse for hire?"

"No," said Henry.

"I'm sorry," said Henry's mother, "we only have the one."

"Perhaps your boy could transport our bags into town?"

Henry bristled. *Your boy?*

"I have to be at the bank by eleven," he said.

"Well then," said his mother, "that'll work out just fine and dandy, won't it, Henry." She whistled for Duke, and his horse responded immediately to her call.

Henry scowled. *Why doesn't Duke come for me when I whistle?*

While Henry struggled with Duke's saddle, Smith studied their home.

"I see you call this Bluebell Cottage." He surveyed the hillside. "I miss the bluebells in spring."

Henry's mother nodded. "I brought acorns from England, and they are doing well." She pointed at a sturdy young oak tree, as tall as a man, growing in the yard. "But most flowers from the Old Country don't seem to grow here."

"New Zealand has its own beauty," said Henry.

"A cruel beauty," she responded.

"I, too, miss England," said Smith. "Especially the parks."

"Yes, we used to stroll through Regent's Park every Sunday," smiled Henry's mother. "Do you remember, Henry?"

Henry muttered and kicked a stone off the path.

"Let's away, Henry," said Smith quietly.

Henry mounted Duke with difficulty, squeezing in front of the visitors' bags, and led the way to the farm gate.

In the garden, his mother watched them leave, then sliced her spade into the ground.

FIVE
THE GANG DRAWS NEAR

"ALL ABOARD!"

On that very same day, some 180 miles further south, three men boarded the steamer *Wallabi* at Greymouth and set sail for more northerly ports.

The men were not out of place among the passengers, some of whom were also roughly dressed and shifty-eyed. But these men had a hunger in their eyes that caused genteel folk to swing wide as they approached.

Their leader was Richard Burgess. Some would call him a pleasant-looking man, but his intense dark eyes could strike fear into the hearts of those who crossed him.

Burgess had spent much of his life in prison in Australia, and was now suspected of robbery and murder in several South Island towns and goldfields.

Travelling with Burgess were his best mate Thomas Kelly, and their newfound partner in crime Joseph Sullivan, recently arrived from Australia. He was a former boxer, a big man with a ready temper.

A fourth man, Philip Levy, had already boarded the boat

but was keeping his distance in order to avoid suspicion. He was a shadowy figure who had never been to prison but lived off the proceeds of other men's crimes. He would befriend unwitting travellers to learn their plans: where they were going, when they were leaving … and how much money they might be carrying. This was useful information for a man like Burgess.

As the steamer chugged its way up the coast, Burgess and Kelly leaned against the rails and shared a flask of whiskey.

Sullivan sidled up to Burgess. "This boat," he said in a low voice, "if it's got any gold … it would be easy to take over."

"I've already 'ad a look around," said Burgess. "There ain't nuffink worf the bovver."

"Well, I'll have a good look for meself," said Sullivan. He cracked his knuckles and walked off.

Kelly scratched his bushy sideburns. "D'you trust that fellow?"

"I don't trust no one 'ceptin' you, me li'l cock sparrer," said Burgess. "Sullivan's a bad man. I'll be keepin' a close eye on 'im, won't I." He grinned and leaned closer. "But I'll tell ya somefink for nuffink," he said. "Sullivan will scruple at nuffink. He's willin' to shed any amount of blood."

Kelly was comforted to hear this. He and Burgess had little regard for human life, and they had a diabolical method of avoiding detection: after stealing a traveller's money or gold, they would "burke" him and hide the body.

Suffocating their victims was a favoured technique. They had done it many times, and it appeared Sullivan would be willing to do the same.

But right now they had run out of money and were looking for a bank to rob. They couldn't stay in Greymouth: the local police chief had heard rumours that Burgess and his gang were planning to ambush a local banker, so he had told Burgess to get out of town.

In three days' time, Richard Burgess and his accomplices would arrive in Henry's hometown, with murderous plans.

Told to get out of town, Burgess and his accomplices headed north on the Wallabi, with plans to rob a bank in Nelson.

SIX

SACRED MOUNTAIN

Doctor Smith, Henry Appleton and Rama left Bluebell Cottage and set off beneath the stark blue sky.

Henry recalled the dull grey skies of London, which, even as a boy, he had found depressing. The dismal smog that hung over the city, and the chimney stacks that belched out their poison breath.

Why would his mother ever want to go back there? The air here in New Zealand was so pure, so fresh!

Henry rode alongside Rama. From the corner of his eye he looked the Māori boy up and down, unsure of what to make of him. Rama stared straight ahead. Henry decided instead to admire the rolling green hills clothed in bush, with stands of giant trees towering over them.

"Kahikatea," he announced. He was determined to learn the names of all these giants. "It's New Zealand's tallest tree."

Doctor Smith made no comment, so Henry added, "It's twice as tall as the Tower of London. Maybe three times."

He detected a small smile on Rama's face, but Smith seemed disinterested.

Henry fixed his gaze on the path ahead, only glancing up when a plump wood pigeon flapped heavily overhead. "Kererū," he said to himself. The noisy beat of the pigeon's wings was a distinctive sound in the forest.

He chuckled as the kererū crash-landed in the upper branches of a titoki tree. It was looking for berries to gorge on. Henry knew it wouldn't find any at this time of year, but there were plenty of other buds and seeds on the bird's menu.

The horses picked their way between the rocks and shrubs and entered a stand of mighty beech trees. Further down towards Nelson township, the settlers had already felled most of the beeches, but up here the trees' remoteness protected them.

Henry smiled at the sunlight filtering through the leaves. "Isn't it beautiful?" He never tired of acting as a tour guide for visitors. "This is Maungatapu – Sacred Mountain."

He was rather proud of his Māori pronunciation, until it occurred to him that Rama actually spoke the language. It didn't seem to matter, though: both Smith and Rama ignored him.

Deep in the forest, it was impossible to ignore the incessant, insistent chorus of thousands of birds above their heads. Not just the familiar repetitive chatter and chirping, but a high-pitched whistling like a bosun's pipe, the rasping of a rusty wheel, the crystal clear tones of a small bell, a deep booming drum call, a child's cry, melodic call signs, high-pitched laughter…

The sound could be quite beautiful. Sometimes the noise drove Henry crazy.

He continued his lecture. "Do you know we have more than 120 species of birds? Maybe 200? Some people…"

Smith broke in with a question. "Is this the path a traveller would take from the goldfields?"

They were at the edge of a stretch of open ground. Not like the gentle meadows of England, but a rough patch of ground dotted with rocks, fern and mānuka.

"Yes, sir," Henry replied. "Canvas Town's in that direction. And Deep Creek."

He guessed Smith would not be interested to hear how his father had worked in the goldfields down there, and how he'd died, and how it had changed Henry's life.

Smith pointed up at the ridge, a few hundred yards away. "So a traveller would proceed from that point… across this open area… and enter the forest there?"

"Yessir. It's the only way." *Why does it matter to him?* Henry wondered.

Without a word, Smith galloped off towards the ridge. Henry looked to Rama for an explanation. But the broad brim of Rama's hat hid his face.

Smith, now a small figure on the ridge, was silhouetted against the painfully bright sky as he checked the lay of the land.

Henry lifted his face to the sun, closed his eyes, and took a deep breath of the fresh mountain air. He recalled the smog of London, and marvelled again that his mother would ever want to return.

Smith galloped back. He said nothing, but nodded at Henry to continue. Henry led the way between the trees.

In a short while, they halted. Looming from the earth beside the path was a giant volcanic rock, bigger than a stagecoach. Henry didn't bother to discuss it. Locals simply referred to it as "the rock" if they mentioned it at all.

"An ideal spot for an ambush," said Smith.

"An ideal spot for an ambush," said Doctor Smith.

Henry guessed that Smith was a military man, always thinking of strategy and tactics. Where he would place his soldiers. Where the horses. Where the cannons.

Henry liked to think of himself as a military man too. *Where would I put my snipers?*

Besides reading cowboy adventures, Henry had read accounts of the bloody battles right here in New Zealand, between Māori warriors and the British soldiers. At Ohaeawai. Ruapekapeka Pa. Gate Pā.

The British had been slow to learn a new style of warfare in the dense forests and rugged hills of New Zealand. They were up against Māori warriors who launched surprise attacks and then melted back into the forest.

Some of the old time British soldiers still insisted on dragging their heavy cannons through the bush and mud and up the slippery hills to pound a Māori fighting pā with their cannon balls.

To their surprise and frustration, when they got there they often found the Māori warriors were long gone.

No, Henry concluded, you had to adapt to a new country. Like Von Tempsky and his Forest Rangers were doing: travelling light, with smaller rifles, ready to fight small groups of Māori warriors in the bush.

He pondered these things as he led Smith and Rama into a new section of dark forest.

The trees were packed together so tightly, as they pushed and shoved for access to the sky, that only a few shafts of sunlight broke through. The horses became skittish. Even the birds seemed subdued.

Henry shuddered.

It was the best of times, it was the worst of times. Dickens' words weren't appropriate to this situation, but somehow they gave Henry comfort.

Finally, they came out into a clearing. Some hard-working soul named Pritchard had spent months felling trees and hacking away the undergrowth to produce a welcome oasis of light.

But at what cost to himself and his family? There was a hand-painted sign that declared *Pritchard's Glade,* but there was nothing to be seen of Pritchard. His cottage, at the edge of the glade, was abandoned.

There was a hand-painted sign, *Pritchard's Glade*, but nothing to be seen of Pritchard. His cottage was abandoned.

On the gate a sign said: *Auction July 12.*

Henry had seen them come and go – bright-eyed immigrants just like his own parents Victoria and William Appleton, willing to work hard but beaten by the weather and debt. And an unfamiliar landscape.

"People are struggling," he said. He was thinking of his mother now, and himself. How would they ever repay the bank and grow enough vegetables to feed themselves? *Maybe I'll go to the goldfields.*

He knew that men died in the goldfields every week:

perhaps drowned while crossing a stream, or ambushed by one of the gangs that preyed on nameless fortune-hunters.

But occasionally a man would emerge with a fortune in gold nuggets.

That could be me, thought Henry. *Henry Appleton, gold prospector, adventurer. Hero.*

SEVEN
HIS FATHER'S GRAVE

Henry led Smith and Rama into open country dotted with cottages and small farms.

He fell silent as they passed the stumps of the hundreds of trees that had been felled for houses, furniture and firewood. Where there had once been acres of flax and raupō, now there was a patchwork of ploughed fields.

Smoke drifted from chimneys and rubbish piles, and the sound of two-man hand saws echoed from the surrounding land.

"Praise my soul, the King of Heaven…" The sound of ragged singing wafted through the clear air.

Just ahead was a small wooden chapel. Two Māori carpenters squatted on the roof, their bare backs glistening in the sun.

This place was special for Henry: his father was buried here.

The sounds of a scratchy violin and singing continued. Henry recognised the Reverend Aloysius Hadfield standing next to two fiddlers, singing lustily but slightly out of tune.

"Ransomed, healed, restored, forgiven…"

On a scarred knoll, an iron fence enclosed a dozen headstones.

The Reverend and a cluster of mourners stood around a fresh grave. Henry wondered whose body had just been lowered into a hole and covered in dirt. It wouldn't be anyone important, because – he looked around – there was only one buggy, and only three horses tethered to posts.

"Ever more his praises sing."

"Henry, laddie!"

The Irish voice belonged to Sergeant John Nash, a man with a kindly face that had begun to wrinkle under the New Zealand sun. He sat on horseback, apart from the mourners. Straight-backed, vigilant, wearing the military cap and blue jacket and trousers of the Nelson Provincial Police Force.

Henry waved and smiled. "Morning, Sergeant, sir." He peered at the sergeant's revolver. It was a Colt .36, the weapon of choice for Wild Bill Hickok – and Von Tempsky.

What he would have given for such a weapon! *Henry Appleton, adventurer. Lawman. Fastest draw in the West.*

"How be your good mother, Henry?"

Henry was still admiring the revolver.

"Henry?"

"Oh – ah, she's well, sir."

"And who might your companion be, Henry?"

Henry looked over at Smith, who was busy scrutinising the faces of the mourners. "Mister Z. Smith, sir."

"Z. Smith?" mused the sergeant.

No need to tell the sergeant anything more. Smith claimed he was a physician, and he had a doctor's bag, but who was to know? Why would a doctor carry a rifle and act so military-like?

Smith looked across at Sergeant Nash and touched his hat. "Sergeant."

Well, at least that's civil, thought Henry.

"An Englishman!" responded the sergeant in his heavy Irish brogue. "Welcome, Mr Z. Smith."

"Praise the everlasting King." The singing stopped.

The mourners removed their hats and bowed their heads. The Reverend Hadfield began a low mumble of prayer.

"Do all these people live hereabouts?" asked Smith.

"Aye," said Sergeant Nash, glancing at the group. "Each and every one."

"So no strangers here."

"Not one. Why do you ask?"

Smith hadn't finished with his questioning. "Who do we bury today?"

"Some poor lad with no name. Here to seek his fortune in the goldfields. Tragic, it is." Sergeant Nash sighed. "Heaven knows I've escorted enough of their bodies back from the fields."

"Cause of death?"

Smith's question was so abrupt and loud that Henry jumped, and a couple of mourners looked up.

The sergeant kept his voice low as he answered. "Drowning, Mr Smith. Like so many. They call it 'the New Zealand death'."

Why don't they learn to swim, Henry pondered, those young men from far away?

"Most of these lads don't know about our fast rivers,

and flash floods," the sergeant continued. He looked over at the graves again. "It's not just drowning, though. Last week, a bullock cart tipped over and crushed poor old Bertie Martin."

Smith grunted and trotted off.

Sergeant Nash shook his head. "The English!"

Henry squirmed. "I'm just taking his luggage," he said.

"Best be cautious until you know a little more about your new friend." The sergeant nodded towards the forest. "Some ne'er-do-wells hide in the shadows, Henry. But others –" he looked at the retreating Smith "– others carry a shadow in here." He tapped his heart.

"I'll be vigilant, Sergeant."

Henry saw Smith had stopped at the chapel. He was saying something to the carpenters on the roof. Now he was going inside.

Henry reckoned he had a few minutes to spare, so he tied Duke to a post and walked with his mother's wild-flowers to a Celtic headstone. He removed his hat and read the familiar words: *Here lies William Henry Appleton, b. 1819 d. 1865.*

Henry bit his lip as he studied the text: *A good man in the eyes of the Lord.*

Certainly William Appleton had been a good man. He'd cared for his family, taught Henry to swim, read him the Bible daily, helped the neighbours build their barn, and made sure there was food on the table. *He was a good father, even though he wasn't my real father.*

What was my real father like? Mother says she doesn't even know his name. Who cares? He didn't love me: he left me. I'm not going to turn out like him. William Appleton is my father. He loved me.

William had even promised to teach Henry to use his rifle. That was before he went off to the goldfields. *Why did he do that? Mother won't let me have the rifle.*

Henry studied the text on his father's grave: *'A good man in the eyes of the Lord.'*

Henry brushed dead leaves off his father's grave, and kicked them away with his boot.

Learn to do good; correct oppression; bring justice to the fatherless. Isaiah 1:17.

The fatherless? he thought. *That's me.* The good man was now a dead man. *Why did he go to the goldfields?*

"Was it my fault?" Henry said aloud.

He realised the sergeant was watching him. So he placed

the wildflowers by the grave, and walked Duke to the chapel.

Rama was on his horse in the shadows beneath a tree. Henry followed the young man's gaze and saw, on a piece of rough ground next to the chapel, a cluster of three graves with small white crosses.

"Tamariki," Rama breathed.

There were words on the crosses in Māori, which Henry could not read. But he could sense the tragedy: three youngsters, probably influenza.

Henry went to the chapel door and peered in. *Where is Doctor Smith?* He spotted him in the front pew, hunched in prayer.

Henry backed out.

On the cemetery mound, the fiddlers were playing a traditional tune as mourners dispersed.

Smith emerged from the chapel. Without a word, he swung himself onto his horse and set off at a clip. Rama followed, and Henry scrambled onto Duke to catch up.

The three horsemen galloped across the open countryside.

What a romantic scene, Henry thought to himself. Someone should paint this picture for the cover of a dime novel. *Henry Appleton and his brave companions. Guns for hire. Soldiers of the prairie. Indian slayers. No, not that. Lawmen. Heroes of the West.*

Henry slapped Duke's muscular neck. *Just like the Wild West,* he laughed to himself. *Why can't I have Father's gun?*

EIGHT
THE TRAFALGAR

They reached Nelson township and slowed to a trot.

The main street, built wide to accommodate turning wagons, was lined with wooden buildings. They were only one or two storeys high, some makeshift but most of them sturdy.

There was a bustle of activity with shoppers and businesspeople; gentlefolk, Māori and European, in formal attire. Tradesmen in work clothes.

Henry wrinkled his nose at the smell from the fresh piles of horse manure that dotted the muddy street. What a change from the fresh mountain air of his farm!

At the door of the butcher's shop, a woman gathered her two young children around her skirts as the strangers approached. Henry could see they were particularly interested in the young Māori man hiding under his wide-brimmed hat.

He was intrigued by Rama too, and was keen to find out about him. For now, however, he was eager to tell the doctor more about his hometown.

"Nelson is on the up-and-up, sir," he called in Smith's direction. "We have ten engineers and surveyors, fourteen shoemakers, fourteen cabinet makers –" he paused for breath "– eleven schoolteachers, fifteen tailors. And seven surgeons."

Smith gave him a look. "How many drinking establishments?"

This momentarily deflated Henry. "Thirty. sir." Why did he want to make a point of that? Some people in Nelson drank a lot of beer and whiskey, certainly, but a lot of folks went to church, too.

An Irish shopkeeper called out. "Top of the mornin', young Henry."

"Morning, Mister O'Shaunessey." *He looks so sad. They say his wife took her own life.*

"You'd be bringin' us some new custom, to be sure?"

Henry grinned and turned to Smith. "He's got five kids to feed." He called back to the shopkeeper in his best Irish brogue: "To be sure, Mr O'Shaunessey!"

Smith said nothing, and scrutinised O'Shaunessey without a smile or a nod as they passed.

Further along, they drew level with a sun-faded hoarding: *The Bank of Nelson. Since 1842.*

"I work here," muttered Henry. He was grateful for the employment, but disliked the people he worked with.

Dodge, the guard, slouched on the veranda. He ignored Henry and glowered at Smith.

Through the uncommonly clean front window Henry could see the unmistakable form of the bank manager, Mister Lester J. Chadwick, staring out at the people of Nelson who needed his money.

Chadwick: a stout, ruddy-faced man in an expensive suit. The man whose bank had once presented Henry with a pony named Duke as a reward for helping catch a bank robber.

The same man who was now threatening to sell the Bluebell Cottage farm.

He's going to sell our home! It's not fair.

Chadwick caught Henry's eye and looked pointedly at his watch. But when Smith gave him a steely look, Chadwick retreated into the shadows. *That's where he belongs,* thought Henry.

Henry stopped outside a large two-storey wooden building that dominated the corner of Trafalgar and Bridge Streets. The Trafalgar Hotel was one of the most impressive buildings in Nelson.

"This is the best in town, sir."

They dismounted. Smith handed his reins to Rama and fossicked in his saddlebag.

Henry spotted something tied to one of the hotel's veranda posts. It was an advertising bill, fluttering in the breeze. Even from a distance, Henry could see two words that set his heart pounding:

Johnny Slick.

Henry gasped. He hurried closer to read more:

TONIGHT ONLY! Hear the remarkable adventures of the United States' most celebrated writer: Mister Johnny Slick.

Henry cried out: "Johnny Slick's in town!" He read on.

A storyteller who has rubbed shoulders with the most famous outlaws and lawmen of America's Wild West. Author of numerous adventure novels, including 'Wild Bill and the Indian outlaw'.

"Henry. My bags?"

Henry picked up Smith's bags, then put them down again. From his pocket, he produced a dime novel and waved it in Smith's direction. "Johnny Slick is my favourite writer, sir."

"He writes penny dreadfuls?"

Henry had to think about that. Dime novels in the United States, but penny dreadfuls in England. Same thing.

"Yessir, they…"

He found himself talking to Smith's back. The doctor had entered the hotel.

Henry turned to Rama, who was still listening. "They're grand stories," he told him.

Rama gave a small smile and dismounted. Henry grabbed the doctor's bag and hurried into the hotel.

The door to Doctor Smith's room was open, so Henry marched in and put down the bags. He was still keen to talk about Johnny Slick, but the doctor was not in a listening mood. He held up his hand. "Please wait."

Henry stepped back and watched as Smith picked up his doctor's bag. Z. Smith. He wondered again what the Z stood for. But now was not the time to ask personal questions.

The doctor pushed aside the stethoscope that lay coiled

on top of other medical paraphernalia, and lifted out a small, ornate jewellery box made of silver. He placed it on the dresser, gently, and next to it laid a Mexican-style crucifix and a silver locket.

He opened the locket and considered it in silence.

Henry stood on his toes to see what the doctor was looking at. It appeared to be a miniature portrait of a woman.

Henry watched as Smith picked up his doctor's bag
and wondered again, *what does Z stand for?*

The doctor closed the locket and rested it on the dresser. Then he produced a purse and handed Henry a coin.

"Thank you, sir."

The doctor coughed and loosened his neckerchief. Henry blinked as he saw a scar around Smith's throat. *Jeepers!* Not a small scar like the one on Henry's shin where he fell on the garden spade, but a jagged scar that snaked from one ear almost to the other.

Henry tried not to stare.

"I appreciate your help, Henry."

Smith held his throat as he talked, and now Henry understood why.

He didn't look to see how much money Smith had given him. He was keen to make the most of his newfound friendship with this man, who was obviously what his mother would call "a man of means".

"sir," he started, "I am extraordinarily motivated to undertake any additional tasks you may have." Henry hoped "extraordinarily motivated" didn't sound too grandiose. *But the Lord knows we need the money.*

"To help my mother," he added. "The farm…"

Smith seemed to understand. "Yes. A heavy responsibility for one so young. Tomorrow morning, then?"

Henry almost hopped on the spot. "Certainly, sir." Then he remembered his proper job, at the bank, under the cold eye of Mr Chadwick. "Oh, flibbertigibbet – I'll be late!"

Smith turned to Rama and smiled. "Flibbertigibbet?" Henry dashed out.

He dragged Duke down the street, hitched him behind the bank, and ran inside to grab the yard broom. Dodge bared his dirty teeth in a snarl as Henry pushed past him and began sweeping the dust from the veranda. Mr Chadwick insisted on having an impeccable frontage "to welcome our illustrious clients".

Henry struggled to push the stiff bristles across the worn timber of the veranda. *This is no place for a famous adventurer,* he told himself. *I should be galloping across the plains, wild and free.* He looked up at the Trafalgar, and was surprised to see Dr Smith at the window. *What's he looking at?* The doctor's gaze seemed focused on something in the distance. Henry – with a glance to make sure Dodge wasn't watching him – tried a small wave.

Smith did not respond. He backed into his room.

Not very friendly. Henry returned to his task, and promised himself a treat after work. He would call on his idol, the visiting American writer Johnny Slick. *Johnny Slick'll be glad to see me.* Two famous writers, talking about their adventures. *And I can ask him about Wild Bill Hickok.*

NINE
A MYSTERIOUS MEETING

The sun was still blazing as the clock down the street struck four. Henry had swept the floors, run a few errands, polished the brass light stands, washed the windows, made a sandwich for Mr Chadwick's lunch, and dusted the bookshelves. Normally, he would stay at the bank a while longer to keep Mr Chadwick happy, but today he had important business. He was off to see Johnny Slick.

He slipped out the door, checked Duke had plenty of water, and ran up the road towards the Rising Sun Hotel.

That's when he saw Doctor Smith stride across the street and enter a well-kept wood and stone building. Although Henry was excited about seeing Johnny Slick, he was also curious to see where the English doctor was going, so he went to the door and poked his head in.

In the subdued light, he could make out a row of bookshelves, and further along there was a crucifix on the wall. *Is this a church? No, can't be.*

He heard the low murmur of voices, and tiptoed a few

steps closer. One of the voices belonged to Doctor Smith. The other – *that's Reverend Hadfield. What are they doing?*

He peered around the corner of the hallway. In a large room lined with dark wooden panels, he saw Doctor Smith sitting on a long bench next to the minister.

"There was a child too?" asked the Reverend Hadfield.

"A child, yes," said Smith. "Unborn."

The minister put a comforting hand on Smith's arm. "How terribly sad."

But to Henry's ears, Smith sounded more angry than sad. "No one has been held to account."

"They will be on Judgement Day," said the minister.

"I can't wait that long."

Reverend Hadfield began: "God says –"

"I know, Reverend. 'Vengeance is mine, I will repay, saith the Lord.' "

"Indeed," said the minister. " 'Be not overcome of evil, but overcome evil with good.' "

Henry nodded. He knew those words too. He peered around the corner again, and saw the two men sitting in silence. They were staring straight ahead at the statue of a gaunt Christ nailed to the cross.

"My friend," said the Reverend Hadfield quietly, "I urge you to pray for the strength to forgive. Not to seek revenge. For your own sake."

"How can I?" Smith jumped to his feet, knocking over a small table.

Henry gasped and backed away. He found himself standing in a small alcove full of musty books and began to shake. He could hear his mother lecturing him, saying,

"Curiosity killed the cat", and wondered how he would explain this latest escapade to her.

But Dr Smith marched past without seeing him.

The startled minister called after the doctor, "Then what do you seek in God's house?"

There was no reply. Henry saw Smith burst from the building and stand on the steps as the townspeople of Nelson shuffled past. A little girl saw him and cried. Her mother scooped her up and carried her away.

Doctor Smith headed off up the street. The Reverend Hadfield slumped to the bench and put his head in his hands. Henry waited a moment, then scurried out of the building.

What was the doctor talking to the Reverend about? A child that died? Revenge?

He stood on the footpath, thinking this over. The doctor had some secrets, it seemed. And to hear a good doctor talking about revenge was worrying. And intriguing.

"Watch out, laddie!" a gruff voice bellowed. Henry realised he had wandered onto the road in the path of a cart, and he jumped out of the way.

Johnny Slick!

Henry put the doctor's mysterious visit out of his mind, and hurried over to the Rising Sun for his next exciting encounter. *What an exciting day!*

This hotel was not as grand as the Trafalgar.

"The Rising Sun is less salubrious," his mother would say. Less *salubrious*… He loved those old-fashioned words, even if he wasn't quite sure what they meant.

Several men holding beer tankards were sitting on a bench,

their feet stretched out. Henry took a deep breath and walked past, avoiding the men's boots. One of them took out his pipe and spat on the path. *Not so salubrious,* Henry thought.

The woman at the front desk was happy enough to give Henry the room number he wanted.

Henry was slightly disappointed. He would have liked to have looked dangerous enough for her to withhold the information. But he was in a hurry, so he simply thanked her and bounded up the stairs.

He whipped out *Masters of the Prairie* and knocked on the door of Room Five. An American voice bellowed: "Enter!"

Henry straightened his collar and hesitated. Could this truly be his hero, the man who had written those legendary books about the Wild West? Was the man who had actually met Wild Bill Hickok now calling for Henry Appleton to enter his presence?

"Be ye not faint-hearted lest the devil take yer throat!" yelled the great man.

Henry gulped and reached for the door handle. He stumbled in, carrying his dime novel.

The curtains were drawn and the room was dark. Henry stopped in the middle of the room and peered into the darkness.

Where is he?

"Mister Slick?" he whispered in a croaky voice.

TEN
TELLER OF TALES

A VOICE BOOMED FROM THE SHADOWS. "AYE, JOHNNY SLICK, teller of tales, friend of the outlaw, feared by…"

The voice stopped. Henry waited.

The voice was now rather matter-of-fact. "Where's ma whiskey?" it demanded.

"Sir?"

A lamp went on. As his eyes adjusted, Henry saw the great writer: large and bewhiskered, draped in an ankle-length coat, sprawled in an armchair.

Johnny Slick! My hero – right here in Nelson!

The American's booted feet rested on a side table, next to an empty whiskey bottle.

"Who are you?"

"Henry Appleton, sir."

Slick tweaked his bushy moustache. "Are you bringing ma whiskey?"

"No, sir. I'm – I came here to meet you, sir." He held out his dime novel. "I've read all your stories, sir."

Johnny Slick slapped his boot. "Goddammit, you're another Western fan. Come to ma lecture tonight."

"My mother wouldn't approve, sir."

As soon as he'd said it, Henry blushed. What kind of adventurer would admit that his mother made the rules?

Johnny Slick roared with laughter. "Your mother wouldn't 'approve'! Ha ha ha."

Henry bowed his head in embarrassment.

As his eyes adjusted, Henry saw the great writer sprawled in an armchair. "I've read all your stories, sir."

"Sonny, I tell ya – some of the most feared outlaws of the Wild West are no older'n you."

Henry knew it. He could name some of them: Jesse James, Jumping Jack Rogers, Cole Younger, Felipe Espinosa…

He peered at this shambolic spectacle – his hero – and decided to press on. After all, he'd come this far.

"Is it true you met Wild Bill Hickok, sir?"

"Wild Bill? Ha ha! Duck Bill, they call him. On account of his 'peculiar features'."

"He killed five outlaws, sir, single-handed."

"Did he now?" Slick seemed surprised, then he guffawed. "Well, if I wrote that, it must be true."

"Sir, how did you become a writer?"

"Questions, questions! Come to ma lecture!"

Henry didn't move.

"Dammit, kid – bring me a bottle and we'll talk." He switched off the light.

Henry had won an audience with his hero.

He wasted no time heading back down the stairs to find a bottle of whiskey for Johnny Slick. He did not like alcohol, or what happened when men drank it, but he was keen to extract as much useful information as possible from the American. *I want to write dime novels too!*

It was only a few minutes before he was rapping on the door to Room Five again.

"Enter, cowboy!" bellowed the American.

Henry was glad the lamp was on as he came back in with the whiskey bottle. He'd charged the cost of the drink to Slick's room, and was proud of himself for being so resourceful.

"Aha!" grunted Slick. "Ma goddam whiskey at last." He grabbed it, wrenched it open, and took a slug. "Ah – the elixir of life, sustainer of hope and courage, fuel for the imagination…"

He gestured at Henry, standing in the middle of the room. "Sit!"

Henry took refuge in a plump armchair and fidgeted with a small rip in the velvet.

Slick held up the whiskey bottle and studied it as if he were about to deliver a Shakespearean soliloquy. With dramatic intensity, he pronounced, "In every bottle, there is one song and a hundred fights."

Such colourful language! marvelled Henry.

"One song and a hundred fights." Slick spluttered and wiped his lips. "That's what them Injuns say anyhow. Very poetic. Wish I'd thought of it."

I'll warrant you'll use it in one of your books anyway.

Slick guffawed and took another slug. Then he turned to Henry. "So you're a wannabe writer."

Henry nodded, eager.

"Righty-right, then," said Slick, and leaned back to enjoy a game. "Once upon a time...?" He gestured for Henry to continue.

Henry gulped. The dime novel fell from his hands. "I ... I ..."

"Come on, kid. Cat got yer tongue?"

Henry crouched to pick up *Masters of the Prairie*. He straightened the cover. Then he cleared his voice. An idea had jumped into his head: an idea straight from his own life.

"Once upon a time," he began, "there was a fatherless young man, desperate to save the family farm. So he decided to rob a bank."

That was impressive, Henry reckoned.

Slick swung the lamp towards Henry and looked hard at him. "Great start, kid. Has this young man got a gun?"

"Yes, sir." *A man needs a gun!* "He's going to steal his father's rifle." Henry couldn't believe that thought came from his own lips. *Steal my father's gun?*

"Swell!" said Johnny Slick. He sat up and took another slug of whiskey.

Henry waited till the coughing stopped, and then added: "I can draw, too, sir." *This is no time to be bashful.* He reached into his jacket and handed over several crumpled sheets of paper, full of sketches of cowboys with blazing rifles.

Slick nodded. "Not half bad, kid." He lay back again and sighed. "You know these yarns are mostly baloney, don'tcha. Hokum."

"That's what my mother says."

"Well, you should listen to 'er, son – whad'ya say your name was?"

"Henry, sir. Henry Appleton."

"Well, Henry Appleton, most of those so-called Wild West heroes are just ornery critters like you and me. 'Ceptin' they're stoopid enough to get a gun an' start shootin' folks."

"But –"

"They mostly die young, Henry. Their flesh ripped apart by pieces of lead." Henry could see that Johnny Slick was sobered up by his own words.

"Then why do you write about them, sir?"

"It's a livin', Henry. A very respectable livin'."

Slick nodded towards Henry's dime novel. "Folks buy them books 'cos they're desperate for heroes. To put a bit o' sparkle in their own drab lives. Poor suckers." He took a drink and mumbled something.

He's drunk! My hero is drunk.

"Sorry to knock the wind outa ya sails, kid." Aware he still had an audience, Slick continued: "I once challenged Wild Bill to a duel."

Great – a story! "Really, sir? What happened?"

"We both missed. We were drunk as skunks." Slick roared with laughter, which ended with more coughing. He took a drink, then leaned forward, serious. "Best advice I can give ya, kid …"

Henry waited. *Yes?*

"Don't write about other people. Write yer own story. And live it."

They stared at each other.

Henry asked, "Live it?"

"Yes. Live it."

Henry saw Slick reach for the bottle again, and decided this was the end of the interview. He stood. "Thank you, Mister Slick."

"For hell's sake, Henry – ma name's Robert Robertson. The Johnny Slick name, sheesh, it's all part of the game. Make-believe."

"Oh," said Henry. *Mother will be pleased to hear this.*

"Nice to meet you, Mr – ah – Robertson." He went to the door.

"Swell meetin' you too, Henry."

Henry reached for the handle.

"Henry!"

Henry turned.

"Henry, have ya heard of this guy ... wassit – Tempsky?"

"Von Tempsky, sir. Yessir, I have."

Henry pulled out his slightly battered *carte de visite* and held it out for the American to study. "He's famous."

"So I hear. A soldier and a painter. May I keep this?"

Henry hesitated. He had traded one of his best sketches for this von Tempsky photograph and counted it among his few personal treasures. But he couldn't say no to this famous author.

"Yessir." He handed it over. "Are you going to write about him, sir?"

"Well ... I'm told he's takin' it easy back home in Auckland right now, so I plan on payin' him a visit when I'm finished here."

"There've been stories about him in the newspapers."

"I've read them. He presents as bein' a bit of a daredevil. They don't tend to make old bones."

"Old bones?"

"They die young, Henry."

"Oh."

Johnny Slick began scribbling in his notebook, so Henry slipped out.

As he stood outside Johnny Slick's door, he heard the legendary storyteller begin to sing: "Early one morn, a young cowboy rode up, A gun in his hand, and fear in his eyes…"

Henry tucked *Masters of the Prairie* in his jacket and turned away. He was still lamenting the surrender of his von Tempsky *carte de visite*, but was excited to have met his larger-than-life hero face to face.

ELEVEN
STRANGERS

"HENRY!"

It was June 10, 1866. A date Henry would never forget. He stood at his bedroom door, yawned, and pulled on a shirt.

His mother, a basket in her hands, was standing next to the photo of her husband, as she often did, with a faraway look in her eyes.

Henry wondered if she was thinking of those happy days in England, when her handsome young husband swept her around the ballrooms of London.

Or the ghastly months at sea, when she was so seasick she cursed the day she had agreed to come to New Zealand.

Or was she thinking of the rain-drenched evening when the men from the goldfields had emerged from the forest with a wagon carrying her husband's body?

"Move the tomatoes, will you please, Henry."

There was work to be done. Always work to be done. Henry sighed, grabbed the sides of the wooden barrel, and rotated it to face the sun.

Despite his moaning, Henry was particularly proud of their tomatoes. He knew no one else in town who grew them, and had no idea where his mother had acquired them. Moreover, she was learning to grow tomatoes in winter, which was quite an accomplishment.

"Three new ones!" he said. They were a rich red, and juicy, and Henry could hardly wait to taste them.

"You can pick two of them for me," said his mother.

She wrapped three eggs in a cloth and placed them in a basket with the tomatoes. "These are for Doctor Smith."

Henry stiffened as he watched his tomatoes disappear. "Why? We need the money more than he does."

"Henry! Doesn't Christ say 'Give, and it will be given unto you'?"

"Yes," said Henry, who had heard Bible verses since he was a toddler. "But Isaiah says 'Bring justice to the fatherless, and plead the widow's cause.' Who's looking after us?"

"We look after ourselves, Henry."

Henry slurped his milk and glared at the basket. "I think I'll go to the goldfields."

"That's no place for an educated young man."

"Father went," Henry retorted.

His mother gave him a despairing look. "And he died there, Henry. Stop it."

The sound of a distant bell reminded Henry he had chores to finish. But he continued to complain to himself as he dragged the saddle onto Duke and prepared his horse for the daily trek to town. *Why me? I should be allowed to write and do drawings. That's my destiny.*

The cottage was picture-perfect in the morning sun. Still

scowling, but enjoying the warmth on his back, Henry climbed onto Duke and arranged the basket on his saddle.

His mother appeared at the door with a spade. She had already worked a good hour in the back garden while Henry slept. "Be back in time for chapel, Henry."

Henry rolled his eyes. "Yes, mother." And he rode off.

He soon forgot his complaints: he was riding free and wild, just like his heroes, the lawmen of the American West. *Ready for adventure. Ready for anything.* Henry grinned as he gulped in fresh air, and tapped the imaginary pistol at his side.

He trotted across the familiar landscape, determined to enjoy the day. Then he yanked his horse to a stop.

Two strangers were sitting by a campfire a short distance ahead.

Both men were muddied and unkempt, like so many of the drifters who travelled the forest tracks linking the small settlements around here. But there was something ... wrong about this pair.

The bigger man had a soulless face, chiselled out of rock. He was squatting on large, dirty work boots and whetting a long knife on a stone.

Next to him, a smaller man flicked the leaves off his velvet and silk waistcoat with shaking hands. "This is the dirtiest, most disgusting, unforgiving, God-forsaken place in all of creation," he snivelled.

"Kelly, shut yer cake hole," said the big man in an Irish brogue. "And stop jitterin'."

The smaller man replied, also in an Irish brogue. "Aye aye, Sullivan." It was clear to Henry that the man could not stop his hands trembling: he tucked them in his pockets.

Henry caught a glimpse of a mermaid tattooed above his wrist.

He pulled Duke's reins firmly to coax him away, and Duke snorted in protest. Both men looked up.

The big man, Sullivan, rose slowly to his feet, holding the knife behind his back.

Henry was accustomed to meeting strangers in these parts, and striking up a conversation. But he did not want to spend a moment longer in the neighbourhood of this pair. He jerked the reins to veer away.

I should have a gun. This thought flashed through his mind as he entered the forest.

Without warning, another man, squat and muscular, stepped out in front of him. Duke reared. The basket flew in the air, and Henry tumbled to the ground, winded. Three eggs, carrots, a cabbage, and the precious tomatoes scattered on the ground.

The man grabbed the reins to restrain Duke. Henry sat up, gasping for breath, and looked at him.

The man was bald, with a bushy moustache and side chops. His muddy clothes had been slept in. But he had a commanding presence.

"If it ain't 'Enry Appleton!" he said.

Henry blinked.

"Yeah, I know who youse are, kid. Done me 'omework."

He clicked his heels together and gave a mock bow. "Richard Burgess, at yer service."

He spoke in the Cockney accent that Henry recognised from his short life in England. He hauled Henry to his feet. "Here ya go, lad. Now 'Enry, I got some questions."

Without warning, a squat and muscular man stepped out in front of him and pulled on the reins. "If it ain't 'Enry Appleton!" he said.

Henry spotted the pistol in Burgess's belt. Despite his fear, he leaned forward for a closer look.

Burgess winked, conspiratorial, and flicked open his coat to allow Henry a good view of the pistol. It was a Colt Army .44 calibre pistol, in bad repair. Henry wondered whether it might not even be in working order.

But although it was not shiny like his father's rifle, or Z. Smith's, or the sergeant's revolver, it was still a weapon, and Henry did not own one.

"For protection, laddie," said Burgess. "A man needs a gun."

Yes! thought Henry, *a man needs a gun.* He began to crawl around to look for any vegetables that had survived. The tomatoes had squashed when they hit the ground.

Burgess handed him the one egg that was still intact. "A good omen, yeah? Heh heh."

"Who's this then?"

Henry looked up to see a pair of dirty working boots in the shadows. It was the Irishman with the chiselled face. Sullivan. "What's he snoopin' round 'ere for, then?" He cracked his knuckles.

The smaller man joined him in the shadows. "D'you know this kid, boss?" he asked.

"Stay out of this, Kelly," said Burgess. Then he addressed Henry in a jovial tone. "Fear not, 'Enry. We are but a merry band of adventurers. London, Australia… an' now New Zealand. We got plans to do business 'ere."

"Master Burgess!" Another man appeared from the shadows, puffing.

Four of them! I'm scared – what are they going to do to me?

The new arrival was tall and bony like Sullivan, but nowhere near as powerfully built. He dressed like a businessman.

"Levy! Welcome back!" cried Burgess. "What news?"

Levy's darting eyes fixed on Henry. He spoke in an educated but reedy voice. "They – ah – the 'party' we're expecting will be here the day after tomorrow."

Sullivan cracked his knuckles and grunted. "We got work to do. Stop pissin' around, Burgess."

Burgess ignored him, and Sullivan retreated into the bushes with Kelly and Levy.

Burgess handed the basket to Henry. " 'Ere you are, lad. Your muvver'll want this." He helped Henry pick up a few carrots. " 'er name's Victoria, innit."

Henry's mouth hung open. *How does he know?* But he dared not ask.

Burgess hoisted Henry onto Duke.

"Thank you – sir." Henry nudged Duke. But the horse did not move: Burgess was still holding the reins.

"I'm guessin' you 'ave a job in town. Eh, 'Enry?"

"Yes sir, the bank…" The moment he had spoken, he regretted it.

TWELVE
IF I HAD A GUN

Henry tried to explain it away.

"Ah – I'm just the cleaner, sir. I sweep. I…" But it was too late.

"The bank, eh? I'll wager they pay you next to nought, eh? Bugger all? 'Scuse me French."

Sullivan returned. "Burgess!" he barked. "Let's be awf!"

"'old yer horses, Sullivan," said Burgess. "I'm just talkin' to our young friend 'ere about 'is job. At the bank." He released Duke's reins. "We'll talk soon, kid. Now awf!" He whacked Duke's rump, and the horse took off.

Henry looked back to see Sullivan, Kelly and Levy dousing their camp fire. There was no sign of Burgess.

Henry cantered through the forest, shaking from his encounter. *The Lord is my shepherd…* He was always on edge under these giant trees that cast such dark shadows, but today was worse. Duke snorted and shook his head.

"It's all right, Duke," he said, trying to calm the horse. But they both jumped when they heard the *snap* of a branch.

Henry looked around, trying to ignore the flickering shapes in the undergrowth. He knew there were no dangerous animals in New Zealand – apart from the occasional wild pigs, and they usually kept their distance.

"Git!" He kicked Duke into action.

They picked their way through the tangle of roots on the forest floor. Henry was thankful that some hardy soul had hacked away the long trails of supplejack vines that once hung in loops from the trees.

He paused at Pritchard's Glade and gazed at the empty cottage with its blunt auction message. He had never met the Pritchards. *Why did they abandon their home? What happened to them?*

Many settlers, just like his mother Victoria, must have wished they had the money to buy a passage back to England. Or Germany, or wherever they came from.

He continued his journey. Those four strangers. *What do they want with us? How did that man know our names?*

He emerged from the forest and saw the cemetery and chapel. The place was deserted. He realised his hands were shaking, and shoved them under his armpits.

He looked back at the forest: dark and brooding.

Are you scared, Henry Appleton? Adventurer – or coward? Henry snorted and climbed off Duke.

In front of the Celtic cross that marked his father's grave, he knelt.

"Father," he began.

He often talked to his father and told him what was racing around in his head. At least his father didn't lecture him like his mother. He just accepted Henry for who he was.

But who is that? Henry asked himself. He didn't feel proud of the way he had dealt with those sinister men back in the forest.

Wild Bill Hickok wouldn't have been afraid. Nor would von Tempsky. They would've stood up to them. Told them to back off.

But then, Wild Bill and von Tempsky always carried a knife. And a rifle. And Henry had neither. He half shut his eyes and asked God to make him stronger.

He squinted at his father's headstone.

… correct oppression; bring justice to the fatherless.

Henry screwed up his face. Was that fair? To be expected to "correct oppression" and "bring justice", when you hadn't even got a gun?

Every sheriff in the Wild West had a gun, and he knew how to use it. Of course, now and then an outlaw who was faster with the pistol would ride into town, and the poor old sheriff would be gunned down in the middle of the dusty street.

Henry shook his head to stop the daydreaming, and stood up.

As he did so, a twig snapped, and he turned around.

Standing there, holding Duke's reins, was Richard Burgess.

THIRTEEN
AN INVITATION

Burgess's chest was heaving as he gasped for breath.

Henry began shaking. He glanced at the forest. *How could he…?*

Burgess answered for himself. "I'm a tough old rooster, 'Enry," he grinned. He paused for breath. "Years of livin' on the road."

He signalled for Henry to come closer. "It's a good life, y'know." He laid a calloused hand on Henry's shoulder. "Master of yer own destiny."

Henry backed away, but Burgess continued his lecture. "You 'eard of Robin 'ood, laddie?"

Henry nodded. Robin Hood and his Merry Men, robbing the rich to give to the poor. Robin's adventures were exciting, although Henry preferred men who had guns, not bows and arrows.

Burgess grinned. "Well, that's us. Robbin' the rich to 'elp the poor."

Henry blinked. This brutish, muddy man was nothing

like Robin Hood, who in Henry's mind would have been a slim, handsome figure dressed smartly in forest green.

"You like that notion, don'tcha?" Burgess enthused. "I can see you're a man of integrity. Like yours truly. We're men of principle."

Don't compare us! a voice shouted inside Henry's head. He tried to look interested, and Burgess continued his chatter.

"I look after me friends. Loyalty, 'Enry, loyalty."

Henry was not sure how loyalty came into the conversation, but he put that thought aside when Burgess placed his hand on Duke's saddle. He was holding his pistol, and Henry couldn't take his eyes off it. But he had a question that was troubling him: *How does he know my name?* He asked it out loud.

"I'll explain later, lad. You an' me gunna do some good work togevva, 'Enry.

Henry shuddered at the thought.

"Meantime…" Burgess shoved his face close to Henry's. "Meantime, don't tell nobody 'bout us, all right. Know what I mean?"

"No," trembled Henry. "I mean yes. Yes, sir." He was still looking at the pistol, and Burgess chuckled. He shoved the weapon into Henry's hands.

" 'Ere, 'ave an 'old. Ain't she sweet?"

Henry, wide-eyed, ran his fingers along the barrel. *A real pistol.* He could sense its power. *Pow, pow!*

"A fing of great beauty in design and mechanics, innit," Burgess purred. "So pretty, but then – BAM!"

Burgess made the sound so loud and percussive that it

could have been a gunshot. Henry jumped, and Burgess laughed.

"Jus' like that, 'Enry, ya can send a man to 'is maker."

Burgess took back the pistol, chuckling. Then, like a panther, he sprang onto Duke. He reached down and held out a hand to Henry. "Now come on, son. I'll give youse a lift into town." He hauled Henry onto the saddle behind him.

Henry wished he could find the words – and the courage – to object. *This is my horse, Duke! How dare you act as if you own him?* But he said nothing.

Burgess stroked Duke's neck with a firm hand. "Been a while since I 'ad an 'orse," he said. "Back in Australia – me 'n' me mates used to travel 'undreds o' miles in a day." He turned in the saddle to grin. Henry pulled back as he saw the man's dirty and broken teeth.

"We'd borrow a nag, ride 'im 'ard for sixty miles, then trade 'im in for fresh legs at the next station."

Henry sniffed. "You mean you stole them."

"Nah, just swapped 'em," said Burgess. "No 'arm done."

They were nearing town, and a young man and woman approached on foot, hand in hand. They veered away as they set eyes on Burgess's muddy clothes. Burgess gave them a cheery wave.

"Ornery folks gimme a wide berth," he chuckled. "Don't worry me none. I prefer me own company. Go where youse like, sleep under the stars." Once again, he turned in the saddle to eyeball Henry. "Life on the road, 'Enry, life on the road. Master of your own destiny. Beholden to nobody. Freedom!"

Freedom? Like Masters of the Prairie! Henry could imagine it. No niggly mother always telling you what to do. No digging the garden. No fences to mend. Just a free and easy life on the road, sleeping under the stars.

Yes, Henry concluded, *here I am, Henry Appleton, riding with a real outlaw. Feared by all.*

Henry wondered whether Burgess had indeed killed a man. He was quite sure he had.

They reached the edge of town and came to a stop as Burgess finished another story.

"An' I said to him, 'Trooper,' I said, 'I respect a man who stands 'is ground under fire. You're free to go.' And awf he went."

"You didn't shoot him?"

"I coulda done," said Burgess. "But I let 'im go, din I. The man had guts. I respect that."

Burgess slipped to the ground and walked a few paces before turning to face Henry. "An' 'Enry, I'm invitin' youse to come join us," he said. He delivered the invitation in a matter-of-fact way, and Henry knew he meant it.

"Howzat, eh? You an' me – jus' like Robin 'ood." Burgess walked off without waiting for an answer.

The way Henry was feeling right now, he probably could have said, "Yes, sir! I will join your gang, I will!" What an honour! *Henry Appleton, part of a feared gang. Free!*

He shifted in the saddle, watching Burgess with a mixture of fear and admiration. Burgess disappeared behind a building.

Is it really a 'gang'? Henry wondered.

Burgess had called it a merry band, but Sullivan and

Kelly didn't look so merry. Probably they would be quite friendly once you got to know them.

Imagine that: Henry standing side by side with the rock-faced Sullivan, inviting anyone – *daring* anyone – to challenge them. *Appleton and Sullivan. And Burgess, and Kelly.*

The gang. *The Appleton gang?* Fearless and free. And armed, all of them.

Henry Appleton with his own pistol.

Henry remembered the basket of food his mother had prepared, still tied to the saddle, and he kicked Duke into action. They trotted into the main street of Nelson. Henry held his head high, shoulders back.

He might not have a gun, but he had *guts*. People would see it.

FOURTEEN
A GIRL

Henry bounded up the stairs of the Trafalgar Hotel and approached Smith's door, carrying the basket.

He lifted the cloth: only one intact egg remained, and he gulped. *Well, he doesn't know how many eggs I started with, does he.* He knocked. *I won't tell him about the tomatoes.*

"Who is it?"

Henry was taken aback. Whose was this light voice?

"It's me, Henry. Is Doctor Smith there?"

The door opened a crack. Eyes scanned Henry, then moved away. The door remained ajar, so Henry nudged it open.

A semi-opaque curtain, strung from wall to wall on a piece of twine, divided the room in half.

Through it, Henry could see the shape of Rama.

So that's who owns the voice. Rama, wearing a cap and baggy jacket, stood at the basin, scrubbing clothes.

Henry placed the basket on the floor. "I brought some … I brought an egg for Doctor Smith." With his boot, he nudged the basket into a corner. *I don't want to be here when he opens it.*

He perched on a chair and got out his well-thumbed *Masters of the Prairie*. But it seemed rude not to acknowledge the person who was in the same room, only a few feet away, so he called out: "You'll never guess who I met."

He had already resolved not to spill the beans about his encounter with Burgess. Nor his spying on Doctor Smith and the Reverend Hadfield.

"Johnny Slick!" Henry waved his dime novel in the direction of the curtain. "The man who writes these cowboy stories. He's amazing. We talked for ages."

There was a muffled response. The sound of running water. Rama obviously didn't propose entering into a discussion, so Henry wandered to the window overlooking the main street.

And there was Doctor Smith himself, striding towards the hotel. Henry opened the window to call out. As he did so, a breeze entered the room, ruffling the partition curtain. For a few seconds, a gap allowed Henry a clear view of Rama, bent over a basin, sleeves rolled up, revealing bare arms.

Rama's arms were slender and smooth. The hands were delicate.

As Rama looked up, Henry saw the face clearly for the first time.

The eyes were soft.

With a shake of the head, Rama released a cascade of long dark hair.

All these images Henry took in fleetingly, as the curtain billowed open.

His jaw dropped as it dawned on him.

A girl! Rama is a girl!

He stumbled backwards and turned to close the window. The curtain settled, and Rama was once more just a diffused shape behind the curtain.

Rama is a girl!

Henry sat and fidgeted. He picked up the dime novel. Stared at it. Put it away. Looked at the ceiling. He began to hum, then hopped up to look out the window again. Studied the clouds.

He spotted the doctor's medical bag tucked in a corner, the lettering Z. Smith barely noticeable. *I still don't know what Z stands for.*

"Henry!"

Henry started. Doctor Smith was in the room.

"Time to pay our respects to the sergeant. Come."

Smith held out the jewellery box to Henry, but Henry was not listening. His mind was whirring. *Why does Rama pretend to be a boy?*

"Henry?"

Henry snapped to. "Yessir!" He took hold of the jewellery box and followed the doctor out the door.

Smith strode ahead of him up Bridge Street. Henry could not resist peering back at the hotel window. And there, looking down at him, was Rama.

He nearly collided with a line of small children, dressed in their Sunday best, trotting after their parents on the way to church.

"Sorry, sorry," he spluttered, and ran to catch up with Smith.

They had to pass the bank on their way to the sergeant's

office. Although the bank was closed to the public today, Chadwick was in his office. He adjusted his bow tie and pulled his long coat around him. Doctor Smith and Henry ignored him.

Henry's mind was whirring with images and thoughts. His terrifying encounter with the Burgess gang – and Burgess's offer for him to join them. Doctor Smith's mysterious conversation with the Reverend Hadfield. And then the discovery that Rama was a girl.

"Henry, your hand, please."

Doctor Smith's voice broke into his thoughts. Henry woke from his daydreaming and realised they were now in Sergeant Nash's small office. Smith had set up an unusual piece of equipment on the old desk crammed with neatly ordered files.

Smith rolled Henry's thumb on an ink pad, then on paper, leaving a clear print of the intricate maze of whorls on Henry's thumb.

"Jeepers!" Henry peered closer at his thumbprint and marvelled at its complexity: a maze of tiny furrows forming a unique map.

Sergeant Nash waited patiently, straight-backed in his military style, and now Smith invited him to roll his thumb on the ink pad too.

Once done, Smith offered him a magnifying glass to compare his print with Henry's.

"Aye, they're markedly different," the policeman acknowledged. "I have read about this, of course."

Smith held his throat in the manner that still fascinated Henry, and said, "Every person on God's earth has a unique signature. The Chinese have known this for a thousand years. Fingerprinting will soon become the most important tool in every lawman's bag of tricks."

Sergeant Nash raised an eyebrow. "You think so? That assumes there's a library with the thumbprints of every criminal in the land. To compare."

"Certainly," said Smith. "But we do already have the print of one particular criminal." From the jewellery box he lifted a small wooden flower press.

Henry recognised the device: his mother had owned one in England, and used it to press the flowers she collected from the riverbank.

Smith took great care as he removed a piece of paper from between the panes of glass. "This," he declared, "is the unique 'signature' of a murderer."

Henry took the magnifying glass and studied the print. "Blood!"

"My own, in fact," said the doctor.

Henry and the sergeant waited for an explanation. Doctor Smith nodded.

"It was two years ago, in Australia," he began.

At last, Henry was about to hear Smith's story. He closed his eyes.

FIFTEEN
ENCOUNTER IN THE DESERT

Henry was blessed with a keen imagination, and he saw everything in clear detail as Smith painted a picture in words.

He could almost feel the heat off the sun-baked dirt as Smith described two figures on horseback galloping across the red desert of Australia.

"A woman had asked me to tend to an injured friend," he said.

Henry imagined the swirl of dust and sand as Smith and a woman in rough working clothes pulled their horses to a stop, outside a small wooden shack standing in the shade of a lone eucalyptus tree.

"As I went in," said the doctor, "I heard the click of a pistol being cocked. An unpleasant welcome.

"It was dark in there, but I could see a man lying on a blanket on the floor. When the woman told him I was the doctor, he put down the pistol – but he left it sitting there right next to him. Obviously a man acquainted with trouble.

"I introduced myself, but he just grunted. Not exactly a friendly fellow.

"Just then, I heard a door creak behind me. I didn't turn round: the less you know in these situations, the better. But I was certain there was someone else there, watching me. Well in fact, I *know* there was.

"We opened the shutters for light, and gave the man a swig of whiskey. I checked his heart.

"And then" – Smith chuckled – "then I brought out my bottle of poison."

"Poison?" asked Henry.

"Yes, that's what was on the label. And my patient was suitably alarmed. 'What the 'ell's that?' he cried. 'Don't worry,' I said, 'I'm not going to make you drink it.'

"I had to explain to him that it was my practice to use diluted carbolic acid to reduce infection."

A small wooden shack in the Australian outback, standing in the shade of a lone eucalyptus tree.

Smith broke from his story to give Henry a medical lesson. "A lot of surgeons still refuse to believe that they carry infection on their bloody hands, from one patient to the next."

Henry nodded. *I'll remember that – if I become a surgeon!*

"So," continued the doctor, "I cleaned my scalpel and tweezers, and told the man, 'This'll be painful.' And he said, 'What do you take me for?'

"So I rolled him onto his side, splashed carbolic acid on the wound, dug out a bullet, and sewed him up again."

Henry shuddered at the thought of needle and thread going through his own flesh. *He makes it sound so easy!*

"And then," said Doctor Smith. "My God!"

Henry and the sergeant sat up. *What?*

"The man's back was crisscrossed with welts and scars. Some of them were still red and raw. I asked him – what on earth…?

"And he said, 'Her Majesty's pleasure.' That's all. Her Majesty's pleasure.

"I assumed the man had been whipped in prison. Best not to ask any more questions, though. I said goodbye – didn't want any payment of course – and left.

"However, just before I left, I made a mistake." He stopped and swallowed. "It cost the life of my beautiful Alicia."

Henry couldn't wait.

"What was the mistake?" he blurted out.

"I told her, 'Fetch me if he needs further help. I'm staying in town.' And I gave her my address: Forty-five, King George Parade."

Smith rubbed his face with his hands.

"I gave her my address. What a fool. I was just doing my job. Being a caring physician."

"Not a fool, surely." It was the sergeant who spoke. Henry saw the policeman's brow was furrowed, and his eyes were locked on the doctor.

"As a physician," said Smith, "one hopes that one's intervention might turn a life around. That the criminal whose life you just saved… may one day prove to have been worth it. The odds are slim, but a physician is sworn to help whomsoever may need it."

He stared at nothing. "I was a fool."

"What happened?" Henry asked, his voice hoarse.

"As I packed up my bag, a man appeared from nowhere, jumped on the woman's horse, and galloped off. She said nothing. And I had no reason to be concerned.

"I gave my horse water, tied on my bag, and set off for home. I was in no hurry."

Smith's voice was dull. "It was night when I arrived back in town.

"As I stopped outside our house I noticed, at the end of the street, the horse that belonged to the woman in the shack. The same horse I'd seen heading off at speed. I was puzzled, of course. But then –"

Henry's heart was thumping so hard he thought the men in the small office would hear it. *And then?*

"A scream," said the doctor. "A terrible scream. It came from our house.

"A most terrible dread came across me. I swear, my heart turned to ice.

"I leapt off my horse. The door was ajar. I kicked it open and pounded up the stairs, three at a time."

"In our bedroom – upturned furniture. A shattered hand mirror.

"On the floor, Alicia's jewellery box.

"A dark shape. A man – rifling through drawers. Pulling out a necklace.

"I didn't care about him. Where was my wife? I stepped into the room, and there…"

This time, Henry did not press the doctor. He did not want to hear the rest of the story.

Smith swallowed and took a deep breath.

"And there – my beautiful wife, Alicia. Lying on the floor. Bleeding. Pregnant with our first baby."

Henry knew she was dead.

"I threw myself down next to her, begging her to stay alive. Begging her."

Henry and the sergeant exchanged glances. They both had tears in their eyes.

"Even as I lay there," Smith went on, 'there was an almighty crash and the intruder charged out of the shadows and made for the door. I could have just let him go … but I was suddenly consumed with a terrible rage. This man had killed my wife.

"I grabbed hold of his boot and hauled on it. He smashed his fist into my face. I didn't let go. I wouldn't let go. We wrestled like animals, ferocious. I had my hands on his neck. He was pounding his fist into my chest. I fought like a demon, and then – suddenly—

"Suddenly, I saw the man's knife flash. It slipped across my neck. There was no pain, but I could feel my blood. Warm on my neck, my chest. I let go. There was no strength left in me. I collapsed.

"The man stood up. 'Bloody hell,' he said. 'Bloody hell.' Then he staggered some, and steadied himself on a cabinet, and left.

"I heard him crashing down the stairs to the street. The sound of horse's hooves …

"That's when I saw it – on the cabinet – clear as day.

"His fingerprint in my blood."

———

In the sergeant's office, Smith was frozen, recalling the events in Australia.

Henry lowered his eyes and imagined how he would feel if his mother had been killed. *Well, I know how I felt when my father died. It's like the end of the world.*

"I just lay there, holding her," said the doctor. "Waiting for death to take me too.

"I could see the man's fingerprint, but I thought – what use would it be? Alicia was dead, and I knew I was dying too."

Silence.

Doctor Smith snapped out of his trance and eyeballed the sergeant.

"The murderer left a fingerprint," he said.

The sergeant's lips moved, but no words came out.

Henry looked up and studied the physician. *So this is the shadow on Doctor Smith's heart.*

Smith's finger traced the scar tissue at his throat. "So you see," he said, quite calm now, "the owner of that fingerprint was the man who killed my wife."

"I am sorry to hear of your tragic loss," said the sergeant.

"He strangled her?"

"Yes, Henry," said Smith. "These men are cold-blooded killers."

Henry was thinking, of course, of Burgess and Sullivan. The men who liked to portray themselves as romantic adventurers. *Was it one of them?* Smith seemed to have no doubts. "Sergeant," he said, "I believe these men are right here in your district."

"How so?"

"I tracked a gang of London criminals from Australia to New Zealand. They were chased out of the West Coast, suspected of armed robbery and murder."

Henry flinched. *Armed robbery? Murder?* Smith was painting a black picture of Burgess's so-called "Robin Hood" gang.

Smith nodded towards the hills. "The gang was travelling in this direction." He began to pack up his gear. "One of them is the killer."

"And he'll face the gallows, to be sure," replied Sergeant Nash.

Henry gulped. *The gallows?* He wouldn't mind seeing Sullivan swinging from the rope, but Burgess ... well, he and Burgess had become friends. In a kind of fashion. Perhaps.

Smith had not finished. He looked straight at the sergeant. "I plan to apprehend the culprit myself."

The sergeant got to his feet. "Doctor Smith, sir — certainly we need good men such as yourself who are willing to stand up for law and order. But taking the law into their own hands? No."

Smith stared at Sergeant Nash. Sergeant Nash stared back.

Henry's mind was a whir. Were his scary friends from the forest genuine adventurers? "Merry men"? Or were they murderers?

You know the truth, said a small voice in his head. *You've met them, you've heard the way they talk, you've seen what they're like.* With that, he stepped forward.

"I've seen them!"

All eyes turned to Henry.

"The men you're looking for," he said. "I know where they are."

SIXTEEN
BACK INTO THE HILLS

ON THE OUTSKIRTS OF TOWN, THE CHAPEL BELL STOPPED ringing. The Reverend Hadfield coughed as he waited for the Luxton family to shuffle into their pew. Then he stood to lead the first hymn.

Outside, a dozen horses tethered to carts nodded in the warm morning sun.

A few children, playing outside in their Sunday best, looked up as Doctor Smith came into view on horseback, riding fast, gripping his Calisher and Terry.

He stopped and waited, impatient, for Henry and Rama, also on horseback. "Show me where!" he shouted.

Henry, panting from the ride, glanced at Rama, who was once again hidden under hat and scarf. "Can't we leave this to the sergeant?" he pleaded.

"No," Smith snapped. "He's made his position quite clear."

Reluctantly, Henry kicked Duke and led the way. They galloped on, past the chapel and the sound of fervent singing.

They passed the cemetery, and Henry glimpsed his father's grave.

Finally, they entered the forest and slowed to a walk. Branches reached out as if attempting to drag them into the shadows.

They reached Pritchard's Glade, and Henry looked about, on edge. The empty windows of the deserted cottage stared back. The three riders trotted into the forest again.

Henry had been wondering all this time, *Am I doing the right thing?*

His mother had a saying: "Out of the frying pan, into the fire." Henry knew things were going to get worse, and he would be right at the centre of it all.

There might be blood. There would certainly be danger.

At least he was spending more time near Rama.

They reached the spot where Henry had been ambushed by Burgess. Henry stopped, embarrassed to see his broken eggs and tomatoes scattered on the ground. They were now swarming with ants and flies.

Rama looked at the eggs, then at Henry, and raised her eyebrows. She slipped from her horse to study the ground.

"The fire's over there," Henry told them.

Smith dismounted and walked to the campfire embers. Rama looked up.

"Four men," she said with certainty.

This impressed Henry. He knew about the American Indian trackers in the Wild West, but he had never heard of a Māori tracker right here in New Zealand.

Without warning, Smith leapt back on his horse. "Stay here. Out of sight." He galloped off.

Henry was taken aback. "Where's he going?"

Rama walked her horse off the track and into the trees. Henry watched her tether her horse under the umbrella of a giant kahikatea, and then looked back at the retreating doctor.

"I have to go," he said. He leapt on Duke and galloped off up the track.

He caught up with Doctor Smith not far away, near the Maungatapu Rock, but stayed out of sight in the shadow of the trees.

He watched as Doctor Smith walked his horse past the rock, his eyes flicking from tree to bush, peering into the shadows and sniffing the air.

A movement on the crest of the hill drew Henry's eye. A group of travellers had appeared, their horses laden with heavy bags. They looked more like businessmen than outlaws, but Smith was interested in them anyway.

The travellers huddled together as he approached, and one man pulled out his rifle.

Smith halted at a distance. "Greetings," he called.

A thin man with a pencil moustache answered. "Bonjour, m'sieur?"

"Ah. Bonjour, messieurs."

Like all educated Englishmen, Smith had learnt French, but he was rusty. "Je m'appelle Smith. Je cherche des hommes – trois hommes." He struggled for the words. "Des hommes 'mauvais'. Bad men?"

The travellers shared anxious looks and shook their heads. "Non, monsieur. Désolé." Two of the men dismounted to adjust their saddles, keeping a wary eye on Smith.

Duke snorted as a light breeze chased dry leaves across

the ground. The breeze whipped some of the leaves into the air around Smith, as if taunting him.

Smith flicked the reins and galloped to the top of the ridge. Henry watched him disappear, then turned to go back to Rama.

He found her squatting on the muscular roots of the kahikatea, and tethered his horse next to hers. "I love this place," he said.

"Where is Doctor Smith?" she asked.

"I don't know. He's gone further on."

He flattened a fern and sat down a respectable distance from Rama.

"Doctor Smith has many worries," she said.

She removed her sandal and took out a twig. Henry was transfixed. He had seen many bare feet, naturally, but … this was Rama's foot.

She looked up.

He turned away.

They were alone, with nothing else to do, so Henry asked the question that had been on his mind for hours. "Why do you pretend to be a man?"

Rama looked deeply into his eyes before answering. "It saves a lot of questions," she said.

Henry frowned. To him, it didn't save any questions at all.

Rama sat next to him and touched his wrist. "Henry. You are a good man. Please tell no one."

Henry studied the hand that lay lightly on his wrist. How could he possibly say no? *She called me a man, not a boy.*

"My name is not Rama," she said. "It is Miriama. 'Drop of the sea'."

Henry knew he had been entrusted with a secret. "Miriama," he repeated. *That's a beautiful name.*

"Horses!" she whispered.

The two of them crouched low and listened to the approaching sounds. Lying in the bracken, Henry was only a handspan from Miriama's face. He savoured the moment. *She is … so beautiful.*

The thud of horses' hooves on hard ground got closer, along with mumbled conversation. On the track just yards from where Miriama and Henry lay, the Frenchmen came into view.

As they trotted past, the thin man peered into the bushes, and Henry was certain they would be seen. But no. Which was just as well, because the man cradling the rifle in his arms was jittery.

Miriama looked into Henry's eyes.

I want to say something to her. But what? His face reddened, and he turned away.

When the Frenchmen had gone, the pair sat up. There was a pause. Henry fumbled with his saddle bag.

Miriama walked away a short distance, and Henry observed her: a slender willow next to a large beech tree. From his saddle bag he took a sketch book and pencil. It had been a long time since he had drawn anything other than cowboys and guns.

Pretending to study the trees, he began to draw Miriama.

SEVENTEEN
FOREST HIDEAWAY

In their forest hideaway, Henry sketched Miriama as she lay half-asleep against a tree trunk.

He would show the sketch to his mother, without fanfare, and tell her how the young "man" who arrived with Doctor Smith had turned out to be a young woman. Rama was now Miriama.

Without warning, Miriama knelt behind him, peering over his shoulder at the drawing. He snapped the book shut. But Miriama smiled and firmly opened it to admire his sketch. Then she looked up. "I want to take you somewhere," she whispered.

"We have to wait for Doctor Smith."

Miriama smiled again. "No, no. We will travel in our minds."

She reached around him, placed a hand over his eyes, and spoke quietly. "It is evening. We are in a waka, just you and me."

A delicious thought! Henry let his imagination run wild.

He could almost smell the salt air and feel the breeze caressing his face.

As Miriama described the scene, she squatted close behind Henry and kept her hand over his eyes. "Can you see it?" she asked.

Henry nodded.

"Our waka is small," she said, "made from tōtara and painted in ochre.

"We dip our paddles without sound. You and me, Henry. Our waka glides across the water. Like a ghost.

"We arrive at a small sandy bay and climb out. You follow me, Henry. Quietly. Up a narrow track through the bushes.

"And here we are."

Miriama paused, her hands still covering Henry's eyes.

"This is my kāinga," she said. "My home."

Miriama and Henry dipped their paddles, and the waka glided ghost-like across the water.

Henry heard the catch in her throat.

"We enter a clearing in the trees and see six whare. Houses.

"There is a garden, but it's overgrown with ferns.

"And a low wooden fence, but some of the fence posts are broken."

Henry gulped as he thought of the fence posts his mother had asked him to fix. *I'll fix them tomorrow. I will, I promise.*

"You haven't told me about the people," he said. "Where is everyone?"

"See over there, Henry? The white crosses, and the monument? That is our urupā. Everyone is gone."

The prow section of a canoe had been upended and 'planted' in
the ground, to form a monument.

Miriama's voice broke. "My aunty, uncle, cousins. My whānau. Everyone."

Her hands still covered Henry's eyes. But they were trembling. "Te Rauparaha?" he asked. "He attacked a lot of villages around here, didn't he?"

He paused.

"Did he kill your family?"

"No," she said. "You did."

Henry brushed away Miriama's hands and turned to face her.

"What do you mean, *I* did?"

"Your people. The English. You brought measles and la grippe."

"Influenza? You can't blame me for that."

"I don't. But the white man's diseases are destroying the Māori people. And the white man's hunger for land."

Henry frowned. "Why do you talk like this? You say 'the white man this', and 'the white man that', but aren't you half-white yourself?"

Miriama nodded. "I am. That is my burden. And my strength. One day I will help to bring the two peoples together."

Henry felt a flash of anger. "Why –"

But Miriama pushed him down, fingers pressed to his lips. "Ssshhh!"

They heard noises, quite close, and shrank back into the ferns. Henry's heart began to thump. *Please God, not Burgess and Sullivan!*

It was not. Two Māori men sauntered past, whacking their sticks at the occasional fern that danced in their way.

Like many of the local Māori men, they were dressed in

the Europeans' white shirts and dark trousers, but their feet were bare. One of them had an ill-fitting waistcoat stretched across his broad chest, and a sailor's cap perched on his head.

The men were followed by three Māori women. Beneath the blankets draped around their shoulders, Henry caught a glimpse of traditional Māori dress.

He was impressed by the size of the loads on the women's backs: one carried an old suitcase, another a few bundles wrapped in blankets and tied with rope. The third, a small sack of potatoes.

Although Henry was guilty of allowing his own mother to do most of the work in their garden, he couldn't help wondering why these men were happy to leave all the load-bearing to the women.

As the group passed, he looked to Miriama for an answer. She frowned. "That is not the life for me," she said firmly.

What is the life for you? Henry wondered.

As if to answer, Miriama lifted her head towards a sliver of blue sky through the treetops. "When I am older, I will travel to England to meet Kuīni Wikitōria."

"Meet the Queen?" Henry laughed. "You can't just march up and say, 'I want to meet the Queen.'"

Miriama ignored him. "After that, I shall return to Aotearoa and teach the children. Teach my people."

"You've got it all worked out," said Henry. His eyes narrowed. *Am I in her dream?*

"Where are your parents?" he asked.

"My mother died when I was a baby."

"Oh. I'm sorry. And your father?"

"Who knows." Her voice was brittle. "He went back to England."

Henry fiddled with his pencil.

"Let us eat," said Miriama, and took bread and cheese from her pack.

"Agh!" Henry yelped. Crouching on his lap, quivering, was an insect the size of a mouse.

It looked fearsome with its large head and jaws, flickering antennae and powerful hind legs.

"Don't move," Miriama told him. She offered her hand to the insect. Henry was aware how calm she was. The insect crawled onto her palm.

"You haven't seen a wētā before?"

"Of course I have. Just not this big."

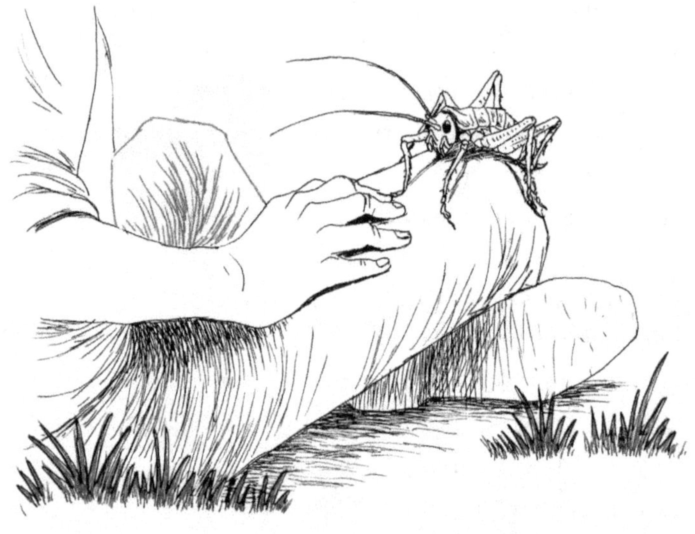

Crouching on his lap, quivering, was an insect the size of a mouse.

Miriama admired the creature in her hand. "Wētāpunga. 'God of ugly things'."

"That's a good name," Henry grumbled.

"I think they're beautiful," she said, placing it carefully on a branch. "The wētā's as old as the mountains."

Henry was annoyed to have been frightened by an insect, and decided to lighten the mood. He jumped to his feet and waved his arms like feelers. "Eek eek eek!"

Miriama put slender hands over her mouth and joined in the laughter. They shared a moment of joy. Then:

"Rama!"

Doctor Smith was back. He frowned at the two giggling youngsters, and their laughter ended abruptly.

"Did you find anything, sir?" Henry asked. *He must think I'm an idiot.*

Smith shook his head. He spied Henry's sketch book and held out his palm. Henry, hesitant, handed it over. Smith studied the portrait of Miriama, and nodded his approval.

"I have a task for you, Henry."

They rode off: Smith leading the way, sitting upright in the saddle, Henry and Miriama following, both flustered from their encounter in the forest.

Henry dared to look at Miriama. She continued to look straight ahead. But there was a small smile on her lips.

EIGHTEEN
HENRY'S SKETCHES

"The face of a killer," said Smith.

Back in Smith's hotel room, the doctor was looking closely at Henry's sketch of Burgess.

"How can you tell he's a killer?"

Henry had heard about the latest craze that everyone was talking about, but could not recall the word. "Do you believe in pre … phre"

"Phrenology? No, no. Phrenology is not good science," said the doctor. "The shape of a man's head has nothing to do with what's in his brain. Or his heart."

Smith tapped Henry's sketch of Burgess. "But I believe this is the man who killed my wife."

Would Burgess do that?

Now Henry resumed sketching Sullivan.

"You have good hands."

"Thank you, sir," said Henry. "I would like to be an illustrator." *Like Johnny Slick. Writing stories and illustrating them myself.*

"Why not a surgeon?" asked Smith.

Henry looked at his hands with new interest. Even his own mother had never suggested such a lofty profession.

A surgeon? Henry liked the sound of it. *Henry Appleton, adventurer. Surgeon.*

Smith took Henry's drawing of Sullivan and examined it. "Excellent. Now our friend the sergeant will have to act."

Henry's mind spun with thoughts of becoming a surgeon, and catching the Burgess gang, and becoming an illustrator …

Then Miriama came into the room.

Miriama!

"Tea?"

Henry realised his heart was thumping again, as he saw Miriama disappear behind the curtain. He watched her diffused figure as she removed her coat.

"Henry?" Smith came closer. "Would you like tea?"

Henry jumped. "Yes! Yes, please. Sir."

Smith unhooked the kettle from above the stove. Henry fussed with his sketch book, watching Miriama's silhouette from the corner of his eye. She splashed water on her neck and shook her head to release her hair. It swirled about her.

"I need to find those men, Henry," said the doctor, handing him a cup of tea. "I'm counting on your help."

He followed Henry's stare and saw Miriama's shadow. His eyes seemed to cloud, and they flicked to the picture of the woman in the locket. He walked to the window and looked out at nothing.

Miriama emerged from behind the curtain, no longer disguised as a man. Henry was aware that he was staring again.

Abruptly Smith turned from the window, and waved Henry away. "Go, go."

What? Henry was bewildered. A minute ago Smith was praising his sketches, and suggesting he become a surgeon, and now…

Miriama opened the door, and gave Henry an apologetic look.

Henry stumbled out, confused, still holding his tea cup. The door closed behind him. *What did I say?*

For a moment he stood there, trying to make sense of his sudden dismissal. Then he thought of Miriama. He put down the cup and bounded down the stairs, onto the street. Grinning, he untied Duke, and was about to mount when Doctor Smith strode out of the hotel, clasping Henry's sketches.

Smith marched up the street. *Where's he going?* Henry was intrigued.

He followed at a distance, leading Duke. Once again they headed along Bridge Street. *Excellent! He's going to show the sergeant my sketches.*

Smith entered the sergeant's office. Henry tethered Duke and went to a side window to peer in.

"Doctor Smith – back again so soon?" said the sergeant. "On the Good Lord's day?"

Smith did not respond, but laid Henry's sketches on the sergeant's desk with a flourish. "These are the men I told you about."

Sergeant Nash looked closely at the sketches. "Did young Henry draw these?"

At the window, Henry smoothed his hair and grinned.

"Yes…" began Smith.

"He has a talent, doesn't he, that boy."

"Never mind." Smith tapped the sketches. "One of these men – at least one – is a murderer."

"They are good sketches, Doctor Smith. But these men have committed no crime that I know of."

"One of them murdered my wife in cold blood."

Sergeant Nash raised his eyebrows. "But the proof?"

"The fingerprint in blood!"

Sergeant Nash picked up the paper with his fingerprint and Henry's. "There's the rub, Doctor Smith. Even if the man's print does match, we still have to demonstrate that you obtained it from the place the crime was committed."

Smith stood up straight and declared solemnly, "I, Zephaniah Smith, give you my word as a gentleman."

Zephaniah! At the window, Henry gasped. At last the "Z" was explained. Zephaniah, a prophet in the Bible. *What a strange name for an Englishman!* Zephaniah, who was squashed between Habakukk and Haggai in the Old Testament.

Sergeant Nash, the tough Irish soldier, tried not to smile at the English "gentleman" standing stiffly before him. "Alas," he said, "your word as a gentleman is not quite enough for a jury."

"God save me!" cried Smith.

At this moment, Miriama joined Henry at the window, a shawl draped over her head and shoulders. She touched his hand and smiled. Henry smiled back, eager to connect, but Miriama was focused on the men in the office.

"So what do you propose?" demanded Smith.

Sergeant Nash shrugged. "I will send a letter to the

police in Sydney for details of their investigation into your wife's death..."

"A letter? Why not a telegraph?"

It was a good question. Henry knew an insulated copper cable was being laid across Cook Strait this very year, to enable the new-fangled telegraph messages to be sent between the South and North Islands. But Australia?

The sergeant smiled. "We are not connected to Australia yet, I'm afraid."

"A letter will take weeks," Smith fumed. "The culprit will be gone."

"Doctor, I cannot send deputies into the hills looking for men who have not committed a crime here. If they come into town we'll keep a watch on them." The sergeant stood. "Meanwhile, Doctor, please do not be tempted to take the law into your own hands."

Smith snorted. "The law? The 'law' seems to have forgotten this crime, Sergeant."

"I understand your frustration. But please be patient. I do not wish to see *you* in court."

Smith turned and marched out. Henry and Miriama were waiting.

"You heard that?" The doctor's face was flushed. "A devil murdered my beautiful wife – and I'm told to have patience."

Miriama placed a hand on Smith's arm, but he pulled away. "He must face justice."

Henry stared at Smith, in awe of his intensity.

"I won't give up until his blood is spilt just like Alicia's," Smith declared.

What? "Sir – you said you would hand him over to the sergeant! Not *kill* him!"

Smith looked at Henry, stony-faced. "You're too young to understand," he said.

Too young? Henry hated the way adults could so easily dismiss someone like him. *As if I don't know the difference between right and wrong.*

Miriama watched with concern as Smith strode off. "The Chinese have a proverb," she said quietly. "Before embarking on a journey of revenge, you should prepare two graves."

"Two graves?" asked Henry.

"One for your enemy, one for yourself," she said. "When a man seeks revenge, he will die too."

Miriama pulled the shawl around her and ran after Smith.

Henry watched, powerless to stop either of them, and angry at being labelled as "too young to understand". He knew what Doctor Smith was planning was wrong. But he did not have the courage to challenge him.

Henry saw Miriama catch up with Smith and walk a few paces behind him. She took a quick glance back at Henry. He raised his hand to wave, but too late. Smith and Miriama had left the street and disappeared around the corner.

NINETEEN
A NARROW ESCAPE

Henry was left standing on the street, wondering if he could have done anything to calm Doctor Smith. *Zephaniah* Smith. But his thoughts became a cascading jumble of worries: his father's death, his mother's frustration with him over farm work, Chadwick and the bank loan to be repaid, people treating him like a boy, his encounter with Burgess and Sullivan, and his attraction to Rama.

Miriama!

The lolling of a church bell somewhere in town woke him from his daydream, and he looked up at the darkening sky. He mounted Duke and trotted off down Bridge Street.

But this was not to be a quiet evening.

As he passed the bank where he worked, Henry was dismayed to see the bulky shape of Mr Lester Chadwick emerge from the darkness.

Henry had no desire to speak to this man, who had put *Auction – Mortgagee Sale* notices on at least half a dozen settlers' farmlets as well as his mother's.

The bank manager caught his eye and Henry had to acknowledge him. "Good evening, sir," he mumbled.

But Chadwick did not respond. He shoved a bulky collection of keys in his coat pocket and headed off down the street.

Henry trotted on, ahead of Chadwick. *Why is it*, he fumed, *that rude men like Chadwick run the world?*

Just when Henry had decided Chadwick was the nastiest man alive, he got a sharp reminder that he was not. Someone else was more to be feared, and that someone was hiding in the shadows at the next street corner.

Protruding into the light were a pair of boots that Henry knew well.

Sullivan! As Henry approached, the boots withdrew into the shadows. *What is he doing here?* Henry held his breath as he rode past the man hiding in the shadows, just a few yards away. *Don't look at him.*

He rounded the next corner into an alleyway and jumped off Duke as fast as he could, dropping the reins. He crept back to the end of the alleyway and peered around.

Chadwick was waddling down the street towards him. And some distance behind, keeping to the shadows, was Sullivan.

He's going to jump him!

Henry pressed back against the wall, breathing heavily. Should he leap out and warn Chadwick – or climb on his horse and flee? He decided instead to follow both men, while he worked out what to do. His heart was pounding, his hands shaking.

They reached a vacant piece of land – by day, a restful

spot for young lovers and children, but by night, full of menace.

The light from a gas lamp threw Chadwick's elongated shadow over the grass as he marched across the park, muttering to himself. Sullivan hurried after him. Henry followed Sullivan. *Should I call out? Will anyone hear?*

Chadwick reached his house, a smart brick and timber cottage that would not be out of place in a well-to-do London suburb. He fumbled with his keys and went inside.

Henry, hiding in the shadows across the road, saw Sullivan creep into the bushes by the front door.

A lantern flickered into life in the front room.

Sullivan reached into his jacket.

He's going to attack him, thought Henry. He looked around for help, but the street was empty. *What can I do?* Should he try to rouse the neighbours? *No time!*

Impulsive, desperate, he stepped out onto the street, and walked towards the house, whistling loudly. *What are you doing?* screamed a voice in his head.

From the corner of his eye he saw Sullivan retreat into the shadows.

Henry bounded up Chadwick's front steps, lifted his shaking hand to the door, and knocked loudly. Sullivan was only a few feet away. *I can hear him breathing.*

The door opened, and Chadwick stood there. "Appleton?"

"Evening, sir," said Henry with a quavering voice. "I have a message from Mister…" As he said these words, he pushed the startled bank manager inside. *What am I doing – assaulting my employer?* Henry was quite surprised at how much strength he could muster as he shoved the big man ahead of him.

"Outrageous!" spluttered Chadwick. "What is the meaning –"

Henry kicked the door shut behind him and pressed his fingers to his lips. "Sir, I'm sorry, but…" He pulled Chadwick by the sleeve into the lounge.

"Let go of me!" Chadwick protested.

Henry, breathless, whispered hoarsely, "Sir, there's a man outside your front door – a dangerous man. I think he plans to steal the keys to the bank."

This news was like a slap across Chadwick's face. He stopped spluttering and glanced at the bunch of keys on the table. "Good Lord!" He strode to a nearby cupboard and wrenched it open.

Henry's eyes widened as Chadwick pulled out a double-barrelled shotgun.

A gun!

"It's loaded," Chadwick told Henry.

"Loaded?"

"Yes, both barrels," snapped Chadwick. He put the percussion caps in place and pulled back both hammers, half-cocked. "Ready to go."

Henry was surprised at the ease with which this portly bank manager, with his soft white fingers, could handle such a lethal weapon. But then, to his delight – and horror – Chadwick thrust it into Henry's hands.

Henry found himself holding a real weapon – a loaded weapon – and was briefly overwhelmed. *I've got a gun!*

The shotgun was new, shiny and beautifully engineered. Deadly. He ran his fingers over the engraved metalwork, noting the unmistakable manufacturer's name, stamped on the barrel in an ornate scroll: *I. Hollis & Sons.*

Chadwick hissed: "Out!" He herded Henry down the hall to the back door, opened it, and pushed him outside. *What are you doing?*

Henry stumbled down the side path towards the street, holding the shotgun, with Chadwick sheltering behind him. *This is crazy!* thought Henry. But what could he do?

As they reached the corner of the house, Chadwick yelled, "Come out, whoever you are!"

Henry stumbled down the side path holding the shotgun, with Chadwick sheltering behind him. *This is crazy!* thought Henry.

Why did he do that? Henry, wide-eyed, pointed the shotgun at the bushes. His finger trembled around the trigger, aware that just a small pressure would send a bullet smashing into the undergrowth.

He waited for any movement. But it seemed Sullivan was no longer there.

Henry was shaking. What if Sullivan *had* been there? *Would I have shot him – or would Sullivan have shot me instead?*

"He's gone, sir," Henry croaked.

Chadwick peered around him to check. "Are you sure there was someone there, boy?"

Boy? He's given me a gun, hidden behind me, but still calls me 'Boy'?

"Positive, Mr Chadwick." *Why am I so polite to this rude man?*

Chadwick grunted. He grabbed the shotgun. "We'll talk about this tomorrow," he said, and headed for the back door.

Henry was left alone, not knowing where Sullivan was – *maybe waiting in the bushes behind me?* But another thought sprang into his head. *The auction.*

The man who had just used Henry as a shield was the same man who was planning to sell the Appleton farm. So despite his nervousness, Henry grasped the opportunity.

"Sir!" he called out.

Chadwick turned around.

"Sir, please don't sell our farm!"

Chadwick snorted. "What a time to –"

"Sir – please give us time. We can earn the money –"

Chadwick turned his back on Henry and yelled over his shoulder. "It's out of my hands." He stepped inside and slammed the door.

At least I tried, Henry consoled himself. *What a horrible man.*

Now Henry's focus returned to his predicament. Somewhere nearby, lurking in the shadows, was the violent man with big boots and a face of rock. Shaking, he looked around at the many shadows that could conceal the big man. *Is he out there, waiting to pounce on me?*

Henry took a deep breath and ran for his life.

TWENTY
TERROR IN THE FOREST

Henry sprinted away from Chadwick's house... *Run!* ... down the street, not daring to look over his shoulder... *Run!* ... across the open ground... and into the alley.

Duke was waiting where he left him. *Thank goodness.* There was no grass there, so the horse was snoozing.

"Duke!"

The animal awoke with a start as Henry charged out of the dark and leapt on his back. "Home, Duke!"

They galloped across the darkening landscape. The last of the sun bathed the clouds in an eerie light.

Henry looked behind him. There was no sign of a large man on a horse in hot pursuit. *I'm safe.* He allowed his horse to slow.

They reached the cemetery, where headstones cast long shadows across the rough dirt. As he always did, Henry glanced over at his father's grave.

What would Father say about all this? What advice would he give? *At least Father had a rifle.*

Henry slowed as they entered the forest to allow Duke to navigate the gnarled tree roots. The exposed roots of the kahikatea, buttressing the tree, looked like the paws of a giant dog.

A forest could be a terrifying place, especially at nightfall. Your worst nightmares took form, hiding behind every tree, rustling the dead leaves…

The dying sun threw long shadows across the forest floor. The forest became a dark cathedral, with pillars of timber and a ceiling of interlaced branches and leaves.

Henry heard the multitude of birds chattering in the trees as they settled in for the night, and there was rustling in the undergrowth as ground-dwelling birds ventured from their burrows.

The further in Henry travelled, the darker it became. An uneasy thought crept into his head. *Is someone following me?* To calm himself, Henry began to hum a vague tune. *The Lord is my shepherd…*

He couldn't help looking around, anxious. Every shadow threatened to devour him. He decided to pray, which was usually a good way to calm oneself.

"Yea, though I walk through the valley of the shadow of death…" he began.

Duke snorted. His hooves scattered the dry leaves and he stumbled over the tree roots.

"Steady, Duke," said Henry, trying his best to sound masterful. *Stay calm.* He shut his eyes and continued the Psalm. "I will fear no evil…"

WHACK! A branch whipped into his face. Henry yelped in pain and let go of the reins to clutch his stinging cheeks.

He grabbed for the reins again, but too late. He lost his balance and tumbled off Duke, crashing to the ground. As he lay there, stunned, Duke eyed him from further along the track.

Henry clambered to his feet, moaning, and rubbing his backside. He hadn't been this sore since Alberta kicked him during milking. He signalled to his horse. "Wait, Duke." *Stay calm. Don't spook the horse.*

There was a rustling movement in the trees.

Henry stared into the dark bushes but could see nothing. *Is someone there? Is it Sullivan?* He stumbled towards his horse, reaching for the reins. *I need to get away!*

"Here, Duke."

He's heard noises too. I mustn't alarm him.

He gestured at his horse. *Come here, Duke!* Duke snorted and trotted a bit further up the track, away from the noises and away from Henry.

"Duke, come back!" Henry yelled. *You stupid animal!* He broke into a sprint to catch his horse.

That was enough to panic the normally placid Duke. He tucked his ears back, kicked up his hooves and scampered up the track, to be swallowed by the dark.

"Duuuuuuke!" Henry cried out.

Now he was alone in the dark forest. Abandoned. His imagination ran riot. The shadows under trees took human form.

Is that Sullivan? Burgess?

Despite his pain, Henry broke into a sprint, scrambling and stumbling over the tree roots.

Under the trees to his left, he was certain he caught sight

of a dark figure. Muscular, catlike, and matching him stride for stride.

Burgess!

"What's the hurry, laddie?" Burgess called to him.

Henry, scared witless, looked to his right and saw those familiar boots, taking huge strides, crushing the ferns. And that chiselled face, twisted and cruel.

Sullivan!

"I don't trust him, Burgess," growled Sullivan.

Henry's imagination ran riot. The shadows under trees took human form.

Henry's feet were flying. *Run, run!*

Sullivan was brandishing a large knife.

He's going to kill me! Henry hurtled down the path. *I don't want to die!*

"I say kill 'im," said Sullivan. "Throttle 'im."

The two men were closing in, their voices terrifying. "Kill 'im!" they barked. "Snuff 'im! Burke 'im!"

Ruuuuuunnnnn!

Henry reached the edge of the dark forest and rocketed out into the open, leaving his pursuers behind in the darkness, and kept running.

Don't stop! He sprinted twenty yards before doubling over, gasping for breath. He dared to look back. The forest was well behind him. *I'm safe.*

A breath of wind ruffled the bushes, and branches creaked and groaned. Henry hoped he had been imagining the voices, but they had seemed so real.

Perhaps they were still there, taunting him? *I'm not going back to check.* When his panting stopped, Henry stumbled on, rubbing his sore bones. *Where is that wretched horse?*

He found Duke near the Maungatapu Rock, nonchalant, feasting on fresh grass.

You good-for-nothing animal! Henry wanted to yell at him, to give him a good telling-off. But he knew that would only alarm Duke and send him galloping off again. As he limped towards the horse he spoke in a soothing voice.

"Good boy," he called through gritted teeth.

Duke stamped his hooves and snorted.

Don't you dare run off, Duke! Henry grabbed the reins. "Don't ever do that again," he said. "Ever." He climbed on his horse, wincing in pain, and they set off, glowing in the pale moonlight.

Now they were in open country.

Henry was still on edge, and glanced behind him to make sure he was not being followed. Maybe by someone on horseback, or maybe someone running. He knew Burgess could do it.

He sighed with relief as Bluebell Cottage came into

view. *Home!* The place he had always felt safe and happy, even in the dark days after his father died. *Wait till I tell Mother everything.*

He saw the comforting glow of a lantern in the window. A wisp of smoke from the chimney. Soon he would be inside, telling his mother how he had saved the rotten bank manager Chadwick, and laughing with her at his scary imaginings in the forest.

In the front yard, he unsaddled Duke. Stretched his sore limbs.

He smiled as he heard a haunting *Für Elise.* Henry knew his mother would be sitting straight-backed at her shiny piano, which they had shipped all the way from England. Her eyes would be closed, her work-calloused hands dancing over the keys.

The piano was one of the few treasures his mother had refused to sell in order to put food on the table. And *Für Elise* was her favourite: a sweet melody that reassured Henry all was well.

But even as Henry reached for the door handle, his mother's playing faltered, and she struck a wrong note. This was strange, because she had played the tune so often she could play it in her sleep.

Something's wrong.

Then he heard a sound that worried him far more. It was the grunting of animals, and it came from their back garden.

Pigs!

The fence! Henry dashed around the side of the cottage to the garden. In horror he saw a section of fence had been knocked down, and a large sow was wallowing in a muddy confusion of uprooted vegetables.

"Get out! Get out!" Henry charged at the animal. The sow struggled to her feet and lumbered back through the fence into Chadwick's field. Two piglets emerged from the mud, squealing, and trotted after her.

Henry did not notice that the piano had fallen silent. He surveyed the ruined garden and slumped to his knees.

What can I say to Mother? No vegetables to eat, and none to sell.

Standing in the doorway, framed by the light, was a squat and menacing figure.

As he knelt in the mud, head in hands, he heard the creak of the back door opening. A shaft of lantern light fell across the garden, and a man called out. "Well, well, 'Enry! Watcha done now?"

Henry froze. He recognized that Cockney voice. *No, no, it cannot be!*

Standing in the doorway, framed by the light, was a squat and menacing figure.

Richard Burgess.

TWENTY-ONE
BURGESS'S BOMBSHELL

Burgess guffawed at the sight of Henry, crouched in the mud. "Your muvva's not gunna be 'appy, lad," he laughed. "Not very 'appy at all."

Henry's mother pushed past Burgess and rushed out into the garden. "Henry!"

"Mother, the garden – I'm so sorry."

But she hugged him. "It is not your fault. Chadwick's men pushed the fence over and chased his pigs in here."

From the doorway, Burgess ordered, "Get inside."

Henry stood, unsteady with anger. "What's he doing here?"

"A man needs a woman's company from time to time," Burgess said, leering. At this, Henry cried out – and charged. Even as he slammed into Burgess, a voice in his head was screaming, *What am I doing? I'm just a boy!*

Man and boy crashed inside. Henry's mother heard the sounds of chairs flying and plates smashing, and hurried after them.

"Henry!"

She found her son and Burgess rolling on the floor, among upturned chairs. In the light from a single lantern, their shadows cast a flickering jumble of dark shapes against the wall.

Henry's arms flailed. Even now, he was thinking, *I'm kinda proud of myself.* But he was no match for the burly outlaw. It crossed his mind that this might be his last day on earth.

"Quit ya fug, boy!" rasped Burgess. He put Henry in a choke hold, and Henry gasped for air. "Tell him to quit kickin'!" Burgess yelled. He jerked his grip tighter. Henry's eyes bulged.

Henry's mother screamed, "Henry – please! Stop!"

Henry, face red, gasping like a fish, stopped kicking.

"That's better," said Burgess, and loosened his grip.

Henry gulped in some air. He was alive, but feeling defeated. His eyes flicked to the photo of his father. *Look what's happening to me! Why aren't you here?*

Burgess kept his arm wrapped around Henry's neck, but his lips were pulled back in a grin, exposing his broken and dirty teeth.

"You're a plucky li'l squirt. But ya need to pick yer fights, sonny. I coulda burked ya, easy."

Burgess addressed Henry's mother, backed against the wall. "I were an 'othead like 'im when I were a boy."

"Henry's a better man than you'll ever be," she retorted.

Mother, please don't make him angrier!

But Burgess wasn't offended.

"I should 'ope so," he replied. "Me own muvva didn't know what to do wiv me." For a moment, Burgess stared at nothing. "Me own muvva," he repeated. "Fink I was born a devil."

He stood and hauled Henry to his feet. "Fix the table."

Mother and son, both shaking, put the chairs in place. Burgess sat at the head of the table and signalled to them.

They sat down side by side, hand in hand. Henry, panting, checked his bruised neck. His backside still hurt too.

Burgess settled the lantern in the middle of the table, then leaned back in a relaxed mode, as if about to tell them a bedtime story.

"I recall – when I were 'bout your age, 'Enry. I were just comin' out of the slammer. And there at the gates, waitin' for me, were me two best friends in the world – me sweet muvva, and me sister Emma." He paused, right in the moment. "And on the uvver side of the road, me mates, come to claim me back as one of their own. I were a pick-pocket back then, 'Enry – one of the best."

Henry's mother had heard enough. "What's this got to do with –"

Burgess silenced her with an upraised hand. He waited to make sure she wasn't going to talk again before continuing. "Course, me muvva and me sister pleaded wiv me, they did. 'Renounce your ways, 'Enry. Choose the God-fearin' parf.'"

Burgess nodded at Henry. "She were a God-fearin' woman, 'Enry, just like yer mum." He chuckled. "Course, I didn't 'renounce me ways', did I. I chose the parf of evil instead."

He looked directly at Henry's mother. "Lookin' back, I blush for very shame."

"Henry would never…"

"Shut up, woman!" Burgess barked. Then, quieter: "If yer don't mind."

Burgess took out his pistol and placed it on the table in front of him. Henry eyed it with mixed thoughts. He had always wanted his own gun, of course, but in the past few days he had seen the way in which bad men used weapons to control good men.

Burgess laid a hand on the pistol. "Now. Some personal business."

From his jacket he pulled a crumpled legal document. Henry had seen one before: it was his father's Will, and it brought nothing but misery. He braced himself for more bad news.

Burgess spread out the document next to the lantern, and spoke in a deliberate, formal voice. "Mrs Appleton. Victoria. Your boy – 'Enry here. 'E's adopted, right? You know that, don'tcha lad?"

"Of course I know," said Henry, putting his hand on his mother's. "This is my mother now."

"Yeah, yeah. Shut up kid." Burgess pointed at the document. "An' 'e were born in London, right?"

They waited…

"On April the 26th, 1851, yeah?"

Henry's mother pulled the document towards her. "Where did you get this?"

"I'll cut to the chase," Burgess went on. "Long and short, 'Enry –"

He paused for effect. Henry waited.

Burgess leant towards Henry. "I'm ya farver."

There was a stunned silence. All that could be heard was

the faint ticking of William Appleton's fob watch on the wall.

"You're my frickin' son, 'Enry," Burgess cried. "Fruit o' me loins."

Henry stared at him, his mind racing. *No! Not this horrible man!*

"I'm yer farver," Burgess insisted. "Your Papa. Daddy."

Henry sprang to his feet. "You're not! You can't be!"

Burgess pressed down on Henry's shoulders. "Sid-down!" He guffawed. "Ain't that the proof? 'E's got the same flamin' temper as yours truly."

"Mother?" Henry appealed to her, but she said nothing, and glanced at the photo of her husband on the wall. Then she held Henry's arm and talked directly to Burgess.

"What was the name of your – lady friend?" she asked.

"Says it 'ere." Burgess poked a finger at the document. "Lizzie. Lizzie Sprickle." There was a hint of genuine affection in his voice.

"Describe her?"

"Short, pretty – much like yerself, Missus. Blazin' eyes."

"Where did she live?"

"Foster's Lane. Number 12. Upstairs."

"What was her trade?"

"Seamstress."

Henry's mother fell silent. He stared at her, waiting.

"I never saw me kid," said Burgess. "Day after Lizzie told me she had a bun in the oven, I were forced to leave town on Her Majesty's business." He jabbed the paper. "Look at this – 'Farver unknown', it says. Huh! Me, Richard Burgess, 'unknown'? "

He sat back, reflective. "I never saw Lizzie after that. Or me kid."

He gave Henry a playful punch. "Till now, yeah?"

Not this man! He cannot be my father! Henry cried out again, "Mother? Please?"

She answered slowly, deliberately. "Your natural mother was a seamstress, Henry. And her name was Lizzie."

"Someone must have told him!" Henry protested.

Burgess laughed. "Look at yerself, kid. Look at me. Peas in a pod."

No, no, no! I cannot be peas in a pod with this man!

Burgess tapped the birth certificate. "Anyway – it's all 'ere."

Henry slumped in his chair, his mind whirring. His mother continued to hold the birth certificate, blank, unseeing.

Burgess picked up his pistol and stood. " 'Enry – outside."

Henry looked at his mother. Pleading. She was staring into space.

" 'Enry!"

Henry shuffled to the door. Burgess pushed him outside and turned to Henry's mother. "Rest easy, 'Victoria'. I ain't gunna to tell nobody about me bein' his farver 'n' all. Don't wanna ruin his prospects now, do we?"

She looked at him, cold. "If you care about him, you'll stay out of his life."

"Wiv respect, ma'am, a farver's got a right."

Burgess left, slamming the door so hard the key fell from the lock.

TWENTY-TWO
GET THE KEYS!

HENRY WAS WAITING OUTSIDE IN THE DARK. BURGESS POINTED to the auction sign that Chadwick had nailed to the front gate. "You and yer muvva, you're in big strife, lad. The bank's gunna sell yer farm right from under yer feet. You. Are. Skewered."

"We're trying to get the money to pay the bank."

"An' how's that comin' along?" Burgess snorted. He leaned forward, conspiratorial.

"Listen, son. Yer farver – the uvver one – he ain't 'ere no more. So I'm gunna take ya under me wing, right?"

Henry shuddered. At this, Burgess patted Henry's cheek. Not hard, but threatening. And again, a bit harder. A slap this time.

"I'm givin' youse a chance to help yer muvver."

"How?"

"We're gunna play a li'l trick on your friend the banker. He's gunna 'and over his gold."

"What?"

"Me band of merry men," Burgess laughed. "We're like

Robin 'ood. Know what I mean? We're gunna take the gold and give it to the poor. And some for youse, 'Enry."

"Robin Hood?" Henry spluttered. This man did not resemble Robin Hood in any way.

"Yeah. Robin flippin' 'ood. You can give your share to yer muvva so she can buy the farm an' all."

"That's… robbery!"

"Course it is, son. But face facts – the bank stole it from youse in the first place. We ain't doin' nuffink wrong."

All Henry could do was quote the Bible. "Thou shall not steal!"

Burgess sneered and, dragging Henry's face close to his own, he lowered his voice. "Everyfink's black an' white for you, innit. But in the real world it ain't so simple."

"But – robbing a bank!"

" 'Enry, stop it! It's a little wrong to balance out a big wrong. See? That's the diff."

Henry thought this over. "I do hate Mister Chadwick," he confessed.

"An' d'you fink your Mister Chadwick gives a rat's arse about you? Nah."

"He says it's 'out of his hands'."

"Out of 'is 'ands, is it? Well, youse 'n' me'll show 'im whose 'ands it's in or out of. Youse an' me, son." Burgess embraced Henry in a crushing bear hug. "This is a proud moment for yer old man, 'Enry."

Henry tried to push him away. "You're not my father!"

Burgess raised his hand as if to slap him again, but stopped. He put his arm around Henry in a friendly fashion. Now he was almost jolly.

"Now, 'Enry. Me mates saw a gentleman this afternoon, riding round in them woods. Very determined, he were."

He waited. Henry said nothing. *They've seen Doctor Smith!*

"You were seen wiv 'im, 'Enry."

Oh, no!

Burgess straightened Henry's collar, casual but menacing. "Who is he?" he demanded. "What's he want?"

"He's a physician." *Tell him everything. He might go away.* "He's trying to find the man who murdered his wife."

Burgess was only mildly interested. "Someone burked his old lady? Well, dumpty-doo. And?"

Henry wondered what else he could say, when suddenly Burgess gripped him. "Tomorra, get us the keys to the bank."

Burgess's eyes flicked to the side of the cottage, and Henry turned to see what had caught the man's attention. He saw nothing but shadows. He turned back to Burgess.

"How can I get the keys? I'm not even allowed to touch them!"

"You'll find a way. Bring them to me."

"So you can rob the bank?!"

" 'Enry, you'll be saving lives," Burgess told him calmly. "Wiv the keys, we can sneak into the bank, quiet and peaceful like. No one gets shot. Uvverwise," and he drew a hand across his neck, "they all die."

With that, Burgess shoved Henry back towards the cottage.

"Meet me tomorra, son. Midday, in Pritchard's Glade. Got that? Midday. Wiv them keys."

Henry limped towards the cottage. He took a few steps

before looking back. Burgess had gone. The cottage door opened and a shaft of light hit Henry. His mother was there, sobbing.

"Henry?"

He fell inside and bolted the door. She hugged him. Henry was ready to cry, but he didn't. *I'm not going to cry. I'm not a kid.*

"That man," she said, "that man is scum."

"But that scum said he's my father. And he might be."

His mother shook her head. "You're not like him, Henry."

But Henry was not convinced. *Maybe I am.* He stood up straight. *Maybe that's not a bad thing. Burgess is tough.* Henry liked that. *Burgess doesn't let people push him around.*

Mother and son stared at each other. Yesterday they had problems – running the farm, trying to pay the bank loan – but those problems seemed trivial now.

Then a floorboard creaked. Henry's mother turned around and screamed.

A dark shape emerged from the shadows. A tall, angular, terrifying man, wearing big work boots.

TWENTY-THREE
SULLIVAN TAKES A HOSTAGE

Joseph Sullivan cracked his knuckles.

"Surprise!" he leered, exposing his rows of rotten teeth. He jumped at Henry's mother and wrapped a sinewy arm around her neck.

Henry cried out, "No!"

"Hear the little rooster crow!" Sullivan raised one large fist and knocked Henry to the floor.

Henry saw stars. A pain shot up his jaw.

"That's for interferin'." Sullivan pressed a large boot against Henry. "I seen youse in town tonight, ya little runt."

Henry lay on the floor, half-conscious. Sullivan's punch had split the skin on his jaw, and it began to bleed. Sullivan prodded him in the ribs with his boot. "Get us the keys for the bank, like Burgess said. Or else."

He pushed Henry's mother out the door. "You're coming with me, lassie." She looked back at her injured son.

"Henry!"

They disappeared into the darkness.

Henry struggled to get to his feet. "Mother!"

"Just get the keys, punk!" Sullivan yelled from the darkness.

Henry staggered to the door, holding his jaw, and peered out into the night. He began to follow them, then reconsidered. He shouted, "Don't hurt her! I'll get the keys." *Somehow.* He closed the front door, and avoided looking at his father's photo on the wall.

I've got to get help. He waited just inside the door, trying to think of a plan. *My head…*

He opened the door a crack. He could see nothing, but the voices carried in the cool night air.

Burgess was out there under the trees. "You shouldna done that, Sullivan," he growled.

"I don't trust that little toad," said Sullivan.

Henry heard his mother say something, and Burgess snapped, "Don't 'arm the woman."

"Aye aye, yer majesty," sneered Sullivan. "Wouldn't dream ov it."

There was the rustling of movement in the bushes. "Move aside, Kelly," said Sullivan.

The sounds receded. Henry leant towards the blackness and listened. *Have they all gone?*

Then Kelly spoke. "You reckon the lad'll do it?"

"Get the keys?" replied Burgess. "Course he will. He's one 'elluva scared kid. C'mon."

A scared kid? Henry bristled. *You wait and see.* He heard Burgess and Kelly follow Sullivan into the forest, then shut the door.

He carried the lantern into his bedroom, set it down, then slumped against the wall. He touched his jaw and winced.

He was a frightened kid, all right. And his head hurt. And his backside. He crawled into the lounge... and collapsed.

He dreamt a scene from *Masters of the Prairie*. He was riding Duke across the wide open spaces, firing his gun in the air, chasing ... or was he being chased? The dream abruptly became a nightmare as he found himself being manhandled by Burgess and Sullivan. Running through the forest. Falling. Being shot. Running again. Burgess's leering face: "I'm yer farver."

He snapped awake. There were birds singing. Dawn light flickered through the window onto his face. He moaned.

I hurt all over. He pushed himself onto his knees, painfully, and peered out.

It was not yet fully light. The leaves in the trees barely stirred. Duke was standing near the cottage, asleep. *I need to get help.* Henry crawled into the kitchen, glanced at his father's photo – *Help me, Father* – and picked three carrots from the vegetable basket.

Keeping low, he crawled to the back door. Outside, he crept to the corner of the cottage, where he could see Duke. He broke off a piece of carrot and hurled it at the horse. It fell short. He got another piece and flung it harder.

PIT! The carrot hit Duke. The horse snorted. He saw the carrot and sniffed it. Chomped it. Henry waved his arms. Duke looked at him, then resumed munching.

Come here, you stupid horse! He waved a piece of carrot in the air. Duke ambled towards him. *That's right, this way.* Henry held out the carrot. Duke took it and munched noisily.

Henry slipped a rope over Duke's neck and led him around the back of the cottage, where they couldn't be seen from the woods. Still on foot, he reached the next field, hidden by the barn. Only then did he risk scrambling onto Duke's back.

We've made it.

He rode Duke bareback, hanging onto his mane and the rope. They walked at a slow pace. Henry realised he was trembling with anxiety, but he had a new focus. *Henry Appleton to the rescue!* He did not dare to think about his mother. *She has to be safe. Please.*

He had no idea where Burgess and his gang might be hiding, so he made as little noise as possible. Duke seemed to understand, and trod lightly along the rough track through the forest.

There was an occasional *whoo whoo* from a ruru about to go to sleep. Other birds were already awake and busy – the kākāriki, pīwakawaka, tūi – even in this moment of intense fear, he found himself trying to recall their Māori names.

Their screeching, trilling, twittering, wheezing, coughing, cackling and chirping was almost deafening.

Henry and Duke entered Pritchard's Glade. It was deserted as always, and Henry tried to avoid the black eye sockets of the cottage's empty windows. He kicked his horse into a trot.

His father's headstone was prominent even in the meagre dawn light, but Henry did not look at it as he trotted past. *I must get help.*

As the sun emerged from the horizon the bright chatter of the birds built to an ear-shattering crescendo. Their warbling was relentlessly cheerful. *If only they knew!*

Henry and Duke galloped on.

Most of Nelson was still asleep when they trotted into town.

It was June 13, 1866.

A lone shopkeeper was sweeping his porch. Henry paid no attention to him, nor to the man sprawled on the sidewalk, hat pulled low. The man watched Henry leap from his horse and run into the hotel.

Henry rapped on the door to Doctor Smith's room. The doctor opened it, holding a shaving cloth to his chin. Miriama appeared behind him, once more disguised as a man.

Miriama. Her face was sad, but she smiled when she saw Henry.

Henry pushed past Smith, gasping. "They've taken my mother!" He collapsed into a chair. "Burgess and Sullivan. They told me to get the keys to the bank. If I don't, they'll kill her."

He buried his face in his hands. "What can I do? They're going to kill her if I tell the sergeant."

Smith placed a hand on Henry's shoulder. "These men must be stopped."

He paused. Then, "Miriama, give Henry your room key."

While she looked for her key, Smith hauled a bag from underneath his bed and took out an object wrapped in cloth. Despite his anguish, Henry watched with interest.

Miriama handed Henry a large door key.

"Henry," said Smith, "take this key to Burgess. Tell him it's for the back door to the bank."

"But he'll find out!" Henry protested.

"They won't go to the bank till nightfall," Smith replied. "That gives me plenty of time to find them."

What? "You're going to look for them?" *What about my mother?*

He was distracted when Smith unwrapped the cloth bundle and pulled out a pair of Tranter revolvers.

The best! Henry was impressed; especially when he saw the guns had pearl handles. Johnny Slick had described a pair in his Civil War novel *Gunfight on the High Plateau*. Why would a respectable doctor have guns with pearl handles? *So flashy!*

Smith shoved a box of cartridges into the pouch on his belt. "I'll start at Pritchard's Glade," he said.

"But when they see you –"

"Henry, stop 'but-but-butting'. I'm an experienced marksman. They're clumsy thugs."

"But there're four of them. I'll come with you." *I'm not a boy anymore.*

"No. That would give the game away."

"What if they kill you?"

"Then you'll make sure the sergeant is waiting for them in the bank." Abruptly, Smith left the room.

Miriama and Henry sat silently for a long moment. They heard the doctor's footsteps retreating down the stairs.

Henry's head was spinning. *It's too dangerous!* "I don't like it."

Miriama squeezed his hand.

The streets of Nelson were still quite empty as Smith rode out of the lane from the stables. He was about to set off when Henry rushed out.

"Doctor Smith – please wait!"

"I've waited too long, Henry."

Henry stood in front of Smith and his horse. "I'm worried about my mother."

"I'm aware of that. Please move."

Henry hung onto the horse's bit. He didn't know what else to do. The horse shied. "Your wife's already dead," Henry cried. "I don't want my mother to die too."

Smith's face was flushed. "Let go, boy!' He slapped his whip on Henry's shoulder. Henry yelped, and released the bit. Smith charged off.

Miriama ran out. "Henry!" She pulled back his collar to see the red welt left by Smith's whip.

Henry scrambled to his feet. "We've got to stop him!"

He was about to untie Duke when an exciting thought struck him. *The rifle!*

Henry was about to untie Duke when an exciting thought struck him. "I need a gun!" he told Miriama.

He bounded up the stairs into Smith's room. The physician's Calisher and Terry was where he'd seen him put it, in the corner next to the wardrobe. He grabbed it and took a box of paper cartridges from the top of the wardrobe. *This is stealing – but I've got to have a gun!*

He raced back down the stairs. Miriama's hand went to her mouth when she saw the rifle, but she said nothing.

"I need a gun!" said Henry. As he untied Duke, he told Miriama, "Find the sergeant! Please! Tell him what's happening."

He jumped onto Duke and galloped after Smith. Miriama watched him go, then headed for the side door. She paid no attention to the bedraggled man still sprawled on the footpath. He got up, cracked his knuckles, and followed her.

As Miriama reached for the door handle, a huge arm wrapped around her.

"You're not going nowhere, sonny," Sullivan grunted.

Miriama cried out. Her hands clawed at Sullivan's jacket. She stamped on his foot and smashed an elbow into his midriff.

Many men would have buckled under Miriama's determined blows. But Sullivan roared like a bull and brought down the handle of his knife on Miriama's head.

She crumpled.

TWENTY-FOUR

HENRY IS CAPTURED

THE SUNLIGHT WAS BEGINNING TO FLOOD THE FIELDS OUTSIDE Nelson when a horse and rider appeared.

Henry Appleton galloped past the chapel, gleaming in the dawn light, and plunged into the shadowy forest. He slowed to allow Duke to find his way through the undergrowth before emerging at Pritchard's Glade.

It appeared deserted, but Henry paused.

"Doctor Smith?" he called. He walked his horse around the perimeter, peering into the shadows, before coming to a stop in front of the cottage. The *Auction* sign hung by a nail, and a loose window creaked.

"Doctor Smith?" Henry called out. His voice was shaky. *I hate this place.*

A pigeon flapped away with heavy beats of its wings.

Where is he? He left town before me, so he must be here somewhere. Unless …

Henry looked at the other side of the glade. *He's probably gone on to the rock.*

He turned his horse, ready to resume his search, when

crack! A twig snapped in the bushes to the right of the cottage.

"Who's there?" cried Henry. He fumbled to reach the physician's rifle which he had slung across his shoulder. As he did so, Burgess leapt out and yanked the horse's reins. Duke reared up, and Henry tumbled off.

Agh! He landed with a thump on his back, and lay where he fell, gasping for air. *That man again!*

Burgess snorted. "Ya need some ridin' lessons, 'Enry."

Henry moaned and reached for the rifle on the ground. *I've got a gun, and I can't even hold onto it.*

Kelly ran from the ferns and grabbed the weapon. "It's not even loaded!" he mocked.

Burgess reached into Henry's coat pocket and pulled out the box of cartridges. "Stupid kid!" he snorted. "You ain't ready to handle a gun."

Give it back! It's Doctor Smith's.

Burgess handed the cartridges to Kelly. " 'ide the 'orse," he ordered.

Henry spluttered as Kelly led Duke away into the bushes. *Why doesn't my stupid horse fight back, like in the Westerns?*

Burgess hauled Henry to his feet and held him tight by the collar of his jacket. "You wasn't meant to come till noon," he said.

Now I'm in trouble, thought Henry. *Think fast!* "Ah – I've got the key," he said. He pulled Miriama's hotel key from his pocket. Burgess grabbed it, frowning.

"The bank?"

Henry nodded.

"Eh? 'Ow come? The bank ain't open yet."

"I went in early," said Henry. *That sounded convincing.*

Burgess eyeballed Henry, still suspicious. "Youse wouldn't dice wiv yer muvva's neck, would ya, kid?"

"No, no," Henry assured him. *Where is she?*

"Master! Someone's comin'!" yelped Kelly from under the trees. Burgess yanked Henry into the ferns, and shoved him to the ground. Then he knelt astride him, with one hand gripped tight across his mouth.

He glared at Henry and drew his hand across his neck. The message was clear: make a noise and your throat will be slit.

Henry spluttered and fought for breath. He heard a horse snort as it approached the cottage. *Who is it? Is it Doctor Smith? Shall I try and warn him?*

Henry screwed his head to one side, and through the ferns he could see the legs of a stallion, stomping at the turf. A boot in the stirrups. *Is it Doctor Smith? Watch out!*

Burgess kept one hand clamped on Henry's mouth, and with other he drew out his pistol. *Oh no – he's going to kill him! What can I do?* Henry squirmed under the weight of Burgess's body. It was useless: Burgess pressed the muzzle of his pistol hard against Henry's cheek and drew his lips back in a threatening snarl. *It's no good – he'll kill us both.*

Smith walked his horse slowly around the side of the cottage.

A bird flapped into the air, and Henry saw Smith climb from his horse, and approach the cottage.

"Kelly's in there!" Burgess muttered as he raised his pistol.

A creak as the back door opened. Then an unexpected sound: a rush of feet nearby, and a scraping and bumping noise as if some large object was being dragged across the ground towards them.

There was a crackle and snap of vegetation as Kelly crashed headlong into the ferns next to Burgess and Henry. He hauled another shape into the ferns alongside him, then collapsed on his back, gasping from exertion.

Henry's eyes popped: the bundle that Kelly had just dumped in the ferns was his mother Victoria. Her hands were bound with rope and a cloth was pulled tight across her mouth.

Mother! She's alive, but…

Neither of them could say a word, but their eyes met in a mixture of fear and relief.

"Good man, Kelly!" chuckled Burgess. He shook his head in disbelief. "Well done!"

Burgess ducked low as Smith emerged from the cottage. "Where are you?" the doctor shouted.

BAM! He fired a shot from his revolver. A bullet smashed through the ferns and whistled past the hidden outlaws. Kelly whimpered and began shaking. Burgess signalled him to stay low. He half-expected the nervous Kelly to burst from his hiding place like a game bird flushed out by hunters. But he stayed put.

Burgess held his grip on Henry's mouth, and Henry tried to use his eyes to signal to his mother: *It's all right. We'll be all right.*

Then … the whinny of a horse … and Smith galloped away. Henry snatched a look. *He's gone back to the rock.*

Burgess waited until the hoofbeats had faded, then released his grip. Henry gulped some air: "Mother! Are you all right?"

She nodded, prompting Kelly to push her head into the ferns.

"Holy Mother," he whined. "That man wants to kill us!"

Burgess snorted. "I've killed plenty like 'im."

Burgess hauled Henry to his feet and told his accomplice, "Kelly, take 'er back in the 'ouse. We need to git goin'."

TWENTY-FIVE
SULLIVAN RETURNS

KELLY TUGGED ON THE ROPES TO MAKE HENRY'S MOTHER stand, and shoved her towards the cottage. Without warning, she turned and head butted him so hard he was sent sprawling.

Burgess roared with laughter. "Attaboy, Kelly!"

Kelly, cussing, scrambled to his feet and grabbed the ropes around his captive's hands. He jerked them hard, and she cried out through the gag.

Mother! Henry could see her wrists were bleeding where the ropes had cut into them. But he had no time to say anything.

"Kelly, 'old onto her!" ordered Burgess. "Tie 'er up nice 'n' tight now."

Kelly half carried, half dragged Henry's mother back towards the cottage. Henry made a half-hearted effort to follow her, but Burgess pushed his arm so far up his back that he cried out in pain.

"Move!" snapped Burgess, and frogmarched Henry

through the trees. Henry looked back to see his mother dragged into the cottage.

Burgess pushed his way through the undergrowth. They marched some hundred yards before they reached a nest the gang had created by trampling down the bracken. Burgess jabbed an elbow into Henry's ribs. "We been forced to 'ide here like rats, 'cos of that doctor o' yours snoopin' around."

"Why don't you leave then, before he finds you," blurted Henry.

Burgess raised his fist, then changed his mind. "There'll be gentlemen 'ere soon wiv gold," he said.

"It's not right!" Henry protested.

"You're such a self-righteous li'l prig, 'Enry! It's 'ard to believe you're me own son."

I'm not your son. Henry looked around. *Where is Duke? And where is Doctor Smith's rifle?* He was horrified to see Kelly join them with a knife and begin to carve his name into the rifle butt.

"Stop it! That's the doctor's!"

"Ooh, that's the doctor's!" Kelly mimicked him, and continued carving.

Henry slumped back in the heather. *How has this happened? A few days ago, all I worried about was the farm. Now Mother and I are both…*

THUMP! A boot struck his chest.

"Aieeeee!" Henry yelped in pain. *My ribs!* He recognized the boots: *Sullivan is back.*

"I shoulda burked ya before!" snarled the big man.

"Lay off, Sullivan." Burgess intervened. "What news?"

But Sullivan didn't pay Burgess any attention. "This

slimy little toad is interferin' with our plans!" He clamped a big hand on Henry's throat. Henry gurgled. "I might just give 'im his ticket o' leave, right now," said Sullivan, tightening his grip.

Henry was bug-eyed. He flung his arms and kicked his legs, but Sullivan was far too strong.

"Get yer 'ands off 'im, knucklehead!" Burgess yelled at Sullivan. He tried to pry Sullivan's hands away, but he could not.

Help! Henry was red in the face and desperate for breath.

"Dammit, Sullivan – he's me son!"

This seemed to get through to Sullivan. "What?" He relaxed his grip but kept his knee on Henry.

Henry gulped in air.

"Watcha mean, he's yer son?" demanded Sullivan.

Burgess put away his pistol. "Me son. God's troof. I bin lookin' for 'im for years."

Sullivan let go of Henry and slammed his huge hands on Burgess's shoulders. "You goin' soft, Burgess?"

Burgess struggled to get free. "Let go, ya fool!"

Henry was wide-eyed as he watched the two accomplices fight.

"Cool it, Sullivan!" yelled Burgess. "We got to work together."

For a moment it looked as though Sullivan would strike his mate. Then he pulled back and let go. "This kid'll turn you in, son or no son," he warned.

He's right, I will! thought Henry.

"No good'll come from snuffin' 'im," retorted Burgess.

I hope he's not my father … but he's saved my life.

"Ye'll regret this," said Sullivan. "Mark me words." He looked at Henry through narrowed eyes. "He knows too much."

Keep away from me!

Sullivan smirked. "Anyway – you ain't gonna talk, are ya, sonny?" He took something from his pocket.

Henry gasped. "Miriama!"

The object Sullivan dangled in front of him was a scarf.

Miriama's scarf.

TWENTY-SIX
EVIL AFOOT

HENRY LOOKED WITH HORROR AT MIRIAMA'S SCARF AS Sullivan waved it in his face. Sullivan curled his lip. "Turns out the doctor's little sidekick is in truth a bird."

Burgess bristled. "We don't 'arm womenfolk, remember?"

Henry believed him. He'd heard Burgess say this before. "We all have muvvas and sisters of our own."

"Back off, Burgess," Sullivan snarled. "No 'arm in a bit o' fun."

What's he done to Miriama?

Sullivan jiggled her scarf in front of Henry again. "Ooh, she's a feisty wee tart!" he taunted.

With dismay Henry saw fresh blood on Sullivan's shirt, and a scratch on his cheek.

Miriama! He couldn't bear to think Miriama had been harmed – or even killed. "What've you done to her?"

"Nothing – yet," Sullivan grinned. "Savin' her for later."

"Where is she?" Henry yelled.

Sullivan hit him, this time with Smith's doctor's bag. Henry fell backwards into the ferns.

"She's safe, as long as you're a good wee boy."

Henry struggled to his knees. He looked past Sullivan and saw Miriama lying unconscious on the ground, hands tied behind her.

"Miriama!" he cried out.

Burgess rounded on Sullivan. "What the 'ell did ya bring 'er for?"

"To make sure he behaves himself."

"We've already got his muvva."

Sullivan smirked. "Quit complainin', yer majesty." He slung Miriama over his bony shoulder and marched into the cottage.

Henry appealed to Burgess. "Don't let him hurt her!"

"You brung this on yerself, 'Enry," said Burgess, and yanked Henry to his feet.

At this moment Levy appeared, breathless. His smart clothes were mud-spattered.

"Comrades!" he called. "What gives?" He saw Sullivan carrying Miriama into the cottage, and frowned at Henry, who was still red in the face. "Too many witnesses!"

"Not for long," Kelly piped up, and drew his finger across his throat like a knife.

Are they really going to kill us? Henry wondered.

Burgess signalled to Levy. "Spill the beans, bruvver."

"They'll be here presently. Three men, five packhorses."

Burgess rubbed his hands. "It's on, lads! Look sharp, Kelly."

Sullivan returned with a leather thong, and secured Henry's hands tight behind his back. He put his craggy face next to Henry's ear and whispered, "Got me eye on you, kid."

Henry shuddered. *God help me!*

The men had found a dark "tunnel" through the dense undergrowth – probably a short cut created by Māori war parties – and they entered it in single file. Levy was up front, followed by Sullivan. Kelly dawdled, humming, carrying the physician's rifle.

Burgess pushed Henry ahead of him through the undergrowth.

Suddenly Levy hissed, "Down!"

Henry gasped as Burgess tugged his thongs to force him to his knees.

"Horseman," said Levy.

Henry peered through the bushes and was alarmed to see Doctor Smith on horseback some hundred paces away.

"It's 'im!" snarled Sullivan.

Doctor Smith stood tall in his stirrups, searching the undergrowth, and yelled, "Come out, you murderer!"

Henry was horrified. *You don't know how close they are! Keep away!*

Smith raised one of his pearl-handled Tranters and fired.

CRACK! A bullet rocketed – WOOSH – through the leaves close to Kelly.

Kelly whimpered. "Why me?"

Shall I call out? Henry wondered. But Sullivan clamped a grimy hand across his mouth.

They huddled behind the bushes: Levy, Kelly, and Burgess and Sullivan, both holding Henry down.

After a time, Burgess peered out. "Gawn," he announced.

"Looks like he's off to Canvas Town," said Levy.

Sullivan removed his hand, allowing Henry to gulp in air. He lay back on the ground, chest heaving. He didn't see Smith ride off. But Sullivan watched keenly.

"That'll keep 'im out of the way while we attend to business," he said. He continued to watch Smith as he rode into the distance.

Burgess looked at Sullivan, quizzical.

Sullivan glared back. "What?"

"D'you know that geezer, Sullivan?"

"What you sayin'?"

"Well," said Burgess, "yer look like ya seen a ghost."

Sullivan grunted. He cracked his knuckles and followed Levy.

Burgess pushed Henry forward, along the rough track towards Maungatapu Rock. It was not long before they emerged from the forest. Sunlight bathed the huge rock.

"A bee-ootiful spot for a pinch o' mischief!" chortled Burgess. "Doo dah bloody doo!"

Henry was reminded of Smith's observation, just a few days ago, that this would be an ideal place for an ambush.

He was about to be proven right.

TWENTY-SEVEN

THE FLAX-CUTTER'S FATE

Burgess hauled Henry behind the rock and sat him down.

"Watch an' learn, 'Enry," he said. "Watch an' learn."

He leaned close. Henry studied the man's facial features. *What ridiculous sideburns! What evil black eyes!*

"You're me son, 'Enry, wevva ya like it or not." Burgess was quiet as he addressed him. Almost gentle. Then he thumped Henry on the arm. "So toughen up."

Agh! Henry slumped back against the rock, sucking his breath against the pain in his arm. *I hate this man!* He watched as they gathered behind the rock.

Kelly caressed his newly acquired rifle. He held it up for Henry to see, pointing at his name carved into the stock, and grinned. *What will I tell the doctor?* Henry wondered. *I probably won't ever see him again, anyway.*

Levy checked his fob watch. Of all of them, Henry thought, Levy seemed the only one who quietly went about his business with no malice. *But he's still part of the gang.*

Sullivan tucked Smith's doctor's bag next to him. Then

he crouched beside Henry, so close that Henry could smell the sweat and dirt on the big man's filthy clothes.

Sullivan pulled out Miriama's beautiful scarf again, and rammed it into Henry's mouth. Then tied his own filthy neckerchief tight over the scarf to keep it in place.

Henry gagged. He took several deep, slow breaths through his nose. *I must stay calm.*

Sullivan turned his attention to Doctor Smith's bag. He ran his rough fingers over it, slowly, as if stroking a piece of silk. Then he stared at the name engraved on it. "Z. Smith?" he grunted. "What the hell?"

He spat, then opened the bag and fossicked through metal instruments and other medical paraphernalia. The stethoscope took his fancy, but he did not know what it was, and twirled it around Henry's head before dropping it back in the bag.

Henry glared at him.

"Ah ha!" Sullivan's eyes widened, and he pulled out a bottle. "Laudanum!" he chortled. "Happy times!"

He looked up to see Henry watching him with tears in his eyes. Sullivan smirked and blew him a kiss.

You monster! Henry resolved right then that he would escape, no matter what. He remembered the cowboy stories he'd read in the dime novels: the hero always managed to break his bonds to free himself. So he shuffled around in the dirt until he could feel a sharp part of the rock behind him, and began to rub his taut leather bonds against it.

Whenever none of the gang was watching, Henry rubbed furiously.

"Listen up, lads," said Burgess, "we got work to do.

Kelly, Levy: stay behind the rock. Keep watch. Sullivan, 'elp me cut a track into the bush."

Sullivan growled: "Aye aye, ya majesty."

Henry continued to rub his bonds.

Henry resolved that he would escape, no matter what.

Knives flashed as Sullivan hacked at the bushes to make a path from the rock into the dark trees. He and Burgess put branches across to hide the entrance.

What are they doing?

Kelly got busy with the physician's rifle, loading a bullet into the breech. He pointed at the weapon, then poked his finger at Henry. "Pow!" He mouthed the word silently, and smirked at Henry's discomfort.

Levy had been on watch, and he cried out, "Someone coming!"

"Every man to his position!" commanded Burgess. All

of them – Burgess, Sullivan, Levy and Kelly – dived behind the rock.

Burgess peered out and grunted. "It's just an old man."

"Gold digger?" asked Sullivan.

"Nah – just a bag o' bones 'n' rags."

But Sullivan was interested in the lone traveller, and he got to his feet. "See for meself," he said. Acting casually, hand in pocket, he sauntered onto the path. Henry strained to hear their conversation.

"Good morning mister," Sullivan greeted the old man. "Fine day."

"Good day, sir." The man sounded nervous – and who wouldn't be, confronted by this tall, rock-faced boxer?

"Ye comin' from the goldfields, old fella?"

"No, sir. Been cutting flax down at Pelorus."

Leave the old man alone, please.

"Cuttin' flax, ya say," Sullivan repeated.

Henry risked a peek over Burgess' shoulder. He saw, up the track, a skinny old man with a swag and shovel.

"Well, I'll be jogging along then," said the old man, and hobbled off down the track.

Thank goodness, they've let him go.

Sullivan dived back behind the rock. "He's got gold, all right!" he said to Burgess.

"Whaddya mean? He's just been cuttin' flax."

"That's his version. Did ya see the way he shifted his knife round the other side when I spoke to 'im?"

Burgess thought this over. "And now he's seen ya, Sullivan."

"Bloody oath! He has, too."

Henry knew evil was afoot. He gave a muffled cry.

Sullivan barked an order – "Kelly, watch 'im" – and hurried after the flax-cutter.

Kelly pointed the rifle at Henry, smirking. Burgess sprang up and followed Sullivan.

Levy cast his eyes upwards. "Good God," he murmured.

They heard Sullivan call out, "Wait up, old man!"

Henry leaned around to watch. The flax-cutter had reached the bushes, but Sullivan grabbed him.

"Let me go about my business!" the old man pleaded. He reached for his knife.

Sullivan held his arm back. "Ye've got gold!"

"No! I've only three pounds cash! Take it!"

But it was no good. Burgess took hold of the old man and dragged him towards the bushes.

Can that really be my father? a voice wailed inside Henry's head.

"Come down 'ere," Burgess ordered the old man.

"D'you want to murder me?"

"What an idea! Course not." Burgess took the old man by the throat.

"I'll go, I'll go!"

Sullivan and Burgess hauled the old man into the darkness of the bushes. Henry slumped back behind the rock, teary-eyed. *Two big men … one frail old man.*

Kelly and Levy looked distressed too. Kelly made the sign of the cross. Lying behind the rock, they heard sounds of a scuffle. The old man screamed,

"Murder most foul!"

Levy grimaced. His hand touched his throat as he imagined what was taking place. Henry, distraught, rubbed hard at his bonds.

"Aaaaghhh!" Henry froze at the cry.

There was a THUMP – the sound of Sullivan's killer punch to the fragile chest of the flax-cutter.

Kelly touched his own chest. Levy flinched and closed his eyes. "God forgive us."

Exactly at that moment, the leather thong holding Henry's hands snapped. He flexed his numb fingers and pulled the strap away from his wrists.

He looked around to take stock of the situation.

Levy and Kelly were both preoccupied. The physician's rifle lay next to Kelly. The doctor's bag was nearby.

Now's the time. Before they get back. He could hear them in the bushes, probably burying their victim. *Now, Henry, now!*

Henry jumped to his feet and grabbed the doctor's bag.

Kelly was gobsmacked. "Whaaa?" He picked up the rifle, but Henry swung the bag hard and knocked the gun out of Kelly's hands.

The rifle hit Levy on the chest. He yelped. "Damnation!"

Kelly scrabbled for the rifle, and Henry did not wait. He ran for his life.

As he fled, he yanked down Sullivan's smelly neckerchief and pulled Miriama's scarf from his mouth.

He charged away like a hunted animal, holding the doctor's bag and Miriama's scarf. *Run, run!*

A dark shape burst from the forest, shovel in hand, in time to see Henry running across the field. Sullivan waved the shovel in the air. "Come back, you little toad!"

Not on your life! Henry kept running.

Levy pointed to the ridge. "They're coming!"

Henry was relieved. *Now they won't chase me!*

Kelly raised the rifle and took aim at Henry, but Levy stopped him. "No! Ye'll give the game away!"

Kelly lowered the gun, muttering.

"The diggers are here!" Levy told him. Kelly peered up the track and saw the distant figures of several men and packhorses.

Sullivan had spotted the diggers too, but he was determined to deal to the skinny kid. "Get him!" he snarled at Kelly as he charged past, pistol in hand. Kelly leapt to his feet and followed with the physician's rifle. He and Sullivan scrambled across the open ground, bent low.

Henry ran wildly, arms flailing, the doctor's bag swinging. *I'm faster! They can't catch me.* Then, abruptly, he stopped.

He was at the top of a steep ravine. Far below was a shallow creek full of rocks.

I'm trapped! What can I do?

Behind him, Sullivan took aim with his pistol. *I'm going to die like a dog!*

Shaking, Henry raised the doctor's bag in front of his chest and closed his eyes.

Sullivan squeezed the trigger.

TWENTY-EIGHT
LIFE AND DEATH

CRACK! THE BULLET WHISTLED THROUGH THE AIR AND smacked into the doctor's bag.

The bag stopped the bullet!

But Henry lost his balance and stumbled backwards. He tumbled down the bank, smashing through bushes, still clutching the bag.

Sullivan and Kelly, panting from their chase, appeared at the top of the ravine and watched Henry fall.

He crashed into the creek, dazed, and crying from the pain. Through blurry eyes, he saw a thin trail of his blood snake into the water. *My blood! My head…*

As Henry lay in the creek, stunned, Sullivan looked back towards Maungatapu Rock. "The diggers!" He peered down at Henry, motionless in the creek.

"He's dead," said Kelly.

"Maybe. Maybe not," said Sullivan. "Git down there an' finish him awf," he ordered, "and get the bag."

Stooped low, Sullivan ran back to the rock. The gold miners were halfway down the slope towards them.

"He looks dead enough," Kelly muttered.

Henry didn't move a muscle. *Please don't come and check on me!*

Kelly examined his precious waistcoat and brushed a sleeve. "Why me?" he complained aloud. "Since Adam was born…"

But he knew better than to disobey Sullivan. Henry listened to Kelly's grunts and cusses as the outlaw began to clamber down the cliff face, slithering towards the creek, using the rifle as support.

Kelly took care to avoid sharp branches: he did not want to damage his waistcoat. But the dirt and clay were slippery, and halfway down his feet shot from under him, and he sat with a thump.

"Oath!" He stood, clutched a branch, and continued to scramble down. Despite his care, a branch snagged his sleeve and ripped it. "Oh, Lordy! That's done it!"

He squinted at Henry in the creek. "Hey!" he shouted.

Henry did not move a muscle. *Play dead!*

His eyes were wide open as he listened to Kelly.

If I keep still, he'll go away.

"Noooo!"

There was a desperate cry from one of the gold diggers. Henry gritted his teeth. The gang had begun their deadly work. Hopefully, Kelly would run back and join them.

"Hey, you!" Kelly called out. Henry heard a clod of dirt sail through the air. Thwack! It hit his head. He winced.

CRACK! The sound of a gunshot echoed across the open space behind Kelly. Henry moved his head very slowly to see whether Kelly was leaving. But the man was becoming more agitated. Henry gasped as he saw him pick up a rock the size of his fist.

Please, no! You'll kill me!

"Hey, kid!" Kelly hurled the rock. Henry waited.

The rock smacked into Henry's leg with a dull THONK.

Aaaaaagh!!! Henry screamed silently. He had never felt such pain. Not even when Duke trod on him that time. *Nooooooo!* The pain shot up his leg. Then back down again. But still he did not move.

He lay crumpled in the stream, fighting to stay conscious, biting his lip till it bled. A jumble of images and thoughts cascaded through his head. Sullivan's hands around his throat. His father's headstone: *bring justice to the fatherless*. The physician's gun.

His longing to have a gun of his own.

My leg hurts so badly. God help me!

I'm going to die and no one will ever find me and —

I'm not even sixteen.

"Noooo!" There was another scream from near Maungatapu Rock, so chilling that it sent startled birds flapping from the foliage. Even Kelly flinched.

The terrible sound unnerved Henry, too. *I can't stand this!* He peered around to see where Kelly was. The man had turned his back on him and begun to scramble back up the slope.

He's going! Henry struggled to his feet. "Aagh!" The pain in his leg was so bad that he could not help crying out loud.

I shouldn't have stood up!

Kelly turned around. "Of all the…!"

Henry cried out as Kelly came leaping back down the

slope towards the creek, wielding the rifle. In his anger and surprise, he forgot his waistcoat as he smashed through the bushes.

Henry scrambled towards the far side of the creek, dragging his injured leg.

Henry scrambled towards the far side of the creek, dragging his injured leg.

Kelly was close behind. He tumbled into the creek, crying out as he thudded into the rocks. "Come back!" He got to his feet, rubbing his shoulder and gasping with pain.

Henry reached the far bank, scooped up the doctor's bag, and clambered up the bank.

"Please, no!" There was another distant sound: a man's anguished cry.

Kelly stopped and glanced back. Then he continued his chase. Henry had disappeared into the dense undergrowth. Kelly charged into the bushes after him.

WHAM!

Henry slammed into Kelly, knocking him off his feet. The rifle he was holding whacked him on the forehead.

"Tarnation!"

Henry turned and burrowed into the undergrowth.

In desperation, Kelly clawed at the rifle, cocked it, and fired into the bushes.

CRACK!

The bullet smashed through the branches only a few feet away from Henry, sending twigs and leaves flying. He stopped in his tracks and gasped. That small lead projectile would have ended his days.

He looked back.

Kelly sat on the riverbank, winded, his clothes torn. "Mother of God…" He peered back up the ravine. "Sullivan'll kill me," he said aloud.

Henry turned away and pushed and clawed his way through the bushes, gritting his teeth at the stabbing pain in his leg.

TWENTY-NINE
HENRY GETS THE GUN

HENRY DROPPED TO HIS KNEES TO COLLECT HIS THOUGHTS. IT was difficult, with the pulsating pain in his leg, but he knew he had to make a plan.

He could no longer see Kelly, but he could hear him. "All right, boyo, you've lost the kid," Kelly muttered. "I can't keep lookin'. He'll be stone dead 'afore too long."

Henry knew this was true. He wanted to lie down right now and die. But he forced himself to push on. He contemplated the steep rise of bush on his left. *I can't climb up that way. I'll circle round.*

He heard Kelly splashing back across the river, cussing and complaining. No doubt using the physician's gun as a walking stick.

Henry picked up a sinewy manuka branch to support his weight, and hobbled in the direction of the Maungatapu Rock. *Dear God, look at me. Help me, please. Give me strength.*

The next hour was a nightmare in which Henry looked down on himself as he marched through the bushes. His injured leg was numb and dragged behind him. The blood had seeped through his trousers. *But I'll make it through.* He had read many cowboy stories about men who carried on after being shot in a gunfight. *And now it's me. Henry William Appleton. Gold prospector, trapper, adventurer. Lawman. Hero of the West.*

He knew he was getting slower. And slower. The bushes were harder to push aside, and his hands were bleeding.

His vision blurred, and he sank to the ground, his chest heaving.

Maybe I won't make it after all. I'll die here in the forest, and they'll never find me. They'll never know what happened. Someone like Johnny Slick would write a dime novel based on Henry's exploits. The story would end with a mystery: where was the famous Henry Appleton? What happened to him? *Maybe they'll find my bones years later. The rats will have eaten me—*

He sat up. There were voices nearby. *I've found them! I've done it! Now I can get the gun back!*

With renewed energy, he dragged himself through the undergrowth, staying as low as he could. Finally, through a screen of ferns, he saw them. The gang. *The murderers!*

They were celebrating the success of their bloody mission. *How many travellers have they killed?*

Kelly was trying his best to be jovial, despite Sullivan's scowls. Soon, however, he had another reason to complain: Burgess put him to work, digging a grave with a miner's shovel.

Henry brushed a pesky fly off his face. He looked around, taking stock of his surroundings like a good secret agent would do. Sullivan and Levy were huddled over a saddle bag, pulling out the contents. Henry saw a handful of banknotes.

Kelly's velvet waistcoat hung from a branch. Once his pride and joy, it was now ripped in several places and splattered with mud.

He pushed the shovel into the soil.

"I don't know why..." he muttered. "The dirtiest, smelliest, toughest, most ignominious, unnecessary..."

Sullivan called out: "Stop whining, Kelly." He held up a small sack and shook it. "Gold," he told Kelly. "You're gonna be rich enough to buy the prettiest waistcoat in town."

They lit a small fire, and Sullivan and Levy began burning papers they pulled from the saddlebag.

"No use for these," said Sullivan.

Henry turned his attention to Kelly, who was leaning on his shovel.

Where has he put the doctor's rifle? Then he saw it – the physician's Calisher and Terry, propped up against a tree. *How can I get it?*

Henry started as Burgess appeared, dragging a body in businessman's clothing. The dead man's heels shuddered as they were pulled across the bumpy ground, and Henry screwed up his face.

"Lend a hand, Kelly," said Burgess.

Kelly scooped up a pile of dirt. "I'm all puffed out," he moaned.

"Lazy sod," said Sullivan.

Burgess, puffing, dumped the body in the grave.

A chill ran down Henry's spine. A short time ago, this 'body' was a living, breathing human being. And now...

The dead man's hat rolled away from his head, revealing a damp patch of – *Blood!* thought Henry. *They shot him in the back of the head.*

He turned away and dry-retched. He'd seen his own father's grey face when they brought his body home from the goldfields, and only last week he had joined the crowds to stare at Bertie Martin's body as he lay crushed beneath his bullock cart. But the man whose body Burgess had just tossed into a shallow grave was different. He had been deliberately put to death by another human being.

Henry peered again at the body, lying face down in the dirt. *They're treating him like a sack of rubbish. It's horrible.* Henry's gaze switched to the physician's rifle. *A man needs a gun to be someone,* said a voice in his head. *Would I ever want to shoot someone this way?*

Today, he had witnessed what happened when men used guns. It was not romantic, like in the dime novels, but grim and ugly.

I still need to get the doctor's rifle, though.

"Kelly, what's this?" cried Levy. "You can see it's a grave from a mile off."

"Don't matter," said Burgess. "We'll be long gone before anyone notices they're missin'." He began piling rocks on the body. "Giz a hand, Kelly." Kelly grumbled and wandered off to find more rocks.

Henry marvelled at how these murderous thugs sounded just like a schoolyard of quarrelling boys. He lay in the thick undergrowth, hardly daring to breathe, and trying to avoid looking at the patch of blood on the dead man's head.

He waited. With Burgess and Kelly busy, heaping rocks

on the grave, and Sullivan and Levy sorting through their bag of stolen goods, Henry saw his opportunity.

He crawled closer to the clearing, still hidden by the bushes, holding his breath, eyes focused on the physician's rifle.

Heart pounding, Henry reached out, grasped the rifle, and inch by inch dragged it across the ground towards him, all the while keeping an eye on the men.

Please don't look up!

He pulled the precious rifle into the bushes, then slithered backwards, furiously, retreating into the forest.

When he could stand, he hobbled away as fast as his throbbing leg would carry him, using the rifle to support him.

It was only a matter of seconds until he heard Kelly's cry: "Me rifle! It's gone!"

"Where was it?" demanded Sullivan.

"Just there. It's gone." Henry could imagine the frantic expression on Kelly's face.

Burgess joined in. "Are you sure you didn't leave it back there?"

They did not sound like schoolboys anymore. These were ruthless men who placed no value on life.

"Kelly," Sullivan growled, "did you finish him awf?"

"The kid? Sure I did."

"You're a bloody liar, Kelly," barked Sullivan.

THUMP! Henry recognized the familiar sound of Sullivan's punch, and Kelly cried out. For a moment, Henry almost felt sorry for him. He hurried away through the bushes.

They'll be after me in a minute.

Despite the twittering of birds, Henry could still hear the men's shouts. "I warned you, Burgess," barked Sullivan. "That kid'll be our undoing. I don't care if he's your son or King Arthur – he's a traitor."

Burgess yelled, "Kelly, go and make sure the women are still tied up."

"Why me?"

"Just go, Kelly," snapped Burgess.

Henry could hear Kelly moaning loudly as he pushed his way through the bushes, and he struggled on, using the rifle as a crutch. But the pain in his leg was draining his strength. He was gasping. The trees seemed to be swimming in the air.

He had gone barely half a dozen paces when his leg gave out. *I can't do it!* He fell away from the path and collapsed into a cluster of ferns. *God help me.*

He was aware of Kelly's grunts and cusses as he approached. And the racket of the birds high above him. His eyes could not stay open. His body demanded rest, even if he was discovered. He held the physician's rifle close to him and allowed sleep to take away the pain.

THIRTY
SHOWDOWN

Fortunately, Kelly's eyes were focused on the narrow path ahead. Muttering and griping, he trudged right past the semi-conscious Henry without noticing him lying flat in the ferns.

Henry struggled to think clearly.

He's going to Pritchard's Cottage! I've got to get up …

He didn't know if he had been asleep for minutes, or seconds. Or even if he had been asleep at all.

Somehow, he stood. Swaying.

God give me strength! He decided he would imagine he was a bird in the trees, looking down on the bedraggled young man staggering through the forest. He would feel no pain. He would simply watch. *No pain.*

He was now on a well-used track through the bushes, and knew it wouldn't be long before he was back at Pritchard's Glade.

Finally, he stepped out of the bushes and saw the abandoned cottage. *I've made it! Henry Appleton, lawman …*

It all seemed peaceful enough. Duke was grazing nearby. A thousand birds were twittering. *Where is Kelly?*

The crunch of boots on dry leaves made him look at the far side of the cottage. There was Kelly, prowling around the building, peering in windows.

Henry did not have the strength to hide. He could only stand, unsteady, fighting off sleep, as Kelly pulled a pistol from his belt and approached the front door.

"Nearly free," came a crystal clear voice from inside the cottage. A woman's voice. *Miriama!*

Kelly stiffened. He crept closer and slipped inside. Henry felt a burst of energy. *I have to do something!* He hobbled as fast as he could towards the cottage.

"Good God!" Kelly exclaimed. "What are you doing?"

Henry peered in the window and saw his mother and Miriama huddled on the floor together, with strands of loose rope around them. Kelly waved his weapon at them. "Lie down, both of you!" he shouted.

Henry sucked in his breath. *What shall I do? Shall I shoot him?*

Shoot him?! Even as these words entered his thoughts, Henry recalled the dead man lying face down in the shallow grave, and the patch of moist blood on his head.

Standing at the window, watching a man waving his gun at the two women he loved most in the world, Henry realised he could not shoot another human being. Not even someone like Kelly, who was himself part of a gang of murderers.

Then he almost laughed at himself: he'd forgotten the rifle was not even loaded. What now? *I don't even have a knife. What would Wild Bill Hickok do?*

Kelly stomped up and down the room. "You don't know what my friends are capable of!" he yelled.

Clunk! Kelly swung around as he heard something bump against the door.

"Henry?" cried Miriama.

It was indeed Henry – still groggy and in much pain, but driven by anger and determined to rescue his mother and Miriama.

He dropped the rifle and leapt like a tiger at Kelly.

Kelly waved his pistol wildly and clawed at the trigger.

CRACK! A bullet shattered the window.

Henry flung his arms around Kelly in a bear hug. *Got you, Kelly.*

"Let me go!" the outlaw cried.

But Henry hung on grimly. He pinned Kelly's arms to his side with the pistol pointing at the floor.

The two women had freed themselves. Miriama picked up an iron frying pan and raised it.

THONK! The pan hit Kelly's skull.

"Agh!" He dropped the pistol. Now Henry's mother was on her feet and struck him with a heavy cooking pot.

CRACK!

Henry let him go, and Kelly collapsed in a heap.

"Miriama! Mother!" Henry fell to the floor. Eyes rolling. *My leg!* He had spent the last remnants of his energy.

He was aware of Miriama calling "Henry!", and everything went black. *Henry Appleton, hero of the West... fatally wounded, and dying in a lonely cabin ...*

He didn't see Kelly struggle to his knees and crawl, moaning, to the door. The two women kept his pistol but let the man go.

Outside, Kelly got to his feet, clutching his throbbing head. "Of all the cruel, unkind, violent..." His voice trailed off, and he disappeared back into the bushes.

THIRTY-ONE
SEARCHING THE DARK HILLS

It was Friday, June 29, 1866.

Richard Burgess had been confident he and his cronies would have several days' grace before their victims' bodies were found. It would give them time to catch a ship to another part of the country, and then on to Australia.

But he was wrong.

The gold miners and businessmen from Canvas Town were reported missing the very next day… and the town formed a search party of volunteers to scour the hills.

The past few days had been tough for the searchers: a storm had lashed the hills, felling trees and flooding the creek. But the men's spirits had been lifted by the discovery of several items they presumed had been abandoned by the Burgess gang – a shovel, a blood-spotted shirt, and a loaded double-barrelled shotgun.

They had also found the body of Old Farmer, the pack-horse that belonged to one of the missing men. The horse had been shot dead.

Rain had been hammering the undergrowth, and ferns bent under the weight of the downpour.

Henry Appleton, no longer able to work on the farm because of his injured leg, had decided to take up his sketchbook again. He sheltered under an oilskin, a walking stick next to him, with his leg stretched out straight.

He peered into the mist, scribbling in his sketchbook as dozens of the good citizens of Nelson joined the police to search the undergrowth.

Henry hoped to sell his sketches to the newspapers.

There were around ninety men in the hills. Some of them were in a human chain, spaced feet apart, looking for clues. They shared a sense of horror and indignation that the peace of their respectable township had been shattered.

Everyone knew, or at least suspected, that the missing men had been murdered.

Henry looked for familiar faces among the searchers. He spotted Doctor Zephaniah Smith and Sergeant John Nash, both on horseback, water dripping from their hats.

Doctor Smith had been very understanding about his Calisher and Terry carbine, and had forgiven Henry for taking it. But he was angry when he saw Kelly's crude signature carved into it, and had taken the gun to a cabinet-maker to remove all traces of the man's name.

If only I could get rid of those names so easily, thought Henry. Burgess and his gang inhabited his dreams every night.

"Miriama!" he called out when he saw her in the rain, searching alongside two elderly Māori men. She was dressed once again in men's clothes, and this time wrapped in an oilskin coat so oversized that it dragged in the mud.

She gave Henry a small wave and kept searching. *She is so beautiful.* Henry found it hard to look away.

"Henry!"

A loud American voice startled him.

He turned to see the bulky figure of Johnny Slick, wearing a cowboy hat and oilskin coat as though he had stepped straight out of one of his Western stories.

"Mister Slick!"

Henry was happy to see his idol again. In the last couple of days, he had re-read some of Johnny Slick's dime novels, hoping to take his mind off Burgess and the murders. It hadn't worked, and Henry knew there was more to come – he was certain that Johnny Slick would write about Burgess's crimes.

The American looked around at the searchers dotted over the hillside. "Just like the Wild West, huh?"

Yes, thought Henry. *But it doesn't seem romantic anymore.*

"Word is, Henry, you're a hero."

Henry shook his head. *Henry Appleton, hero?* "No, no." *I used to want that. Not now.*

"Well…" drawled the American, "ya bin kidnapped and shot, broke ya leg, rescued ya womenfolk, and helped track down a bunch o' vermin. Sure sounds like a hero to me."

"I'm just glad to be alive," mumbled Henry.

Slick slapped him on the back.

"Good on ya, kid. Ya bin writin' your own story. Just like I told ya."

He moved away, and Henry pondered his words. *He called me a kid, yes. But treated me like a man.*

Then, up in the bush-clad slopes, a bugle sounded the Officer's Call. Its no-nonsense military summons was oddly out of place as it echoed around the hills, but men came running.

A body had been found.

Searchers converged on the spot, and Henry joined them. It was not long before there were more grisly discoveries.

Henry's pencil recorded it all: the ugly handiwork of four of God's creatures – Richard Burgess, Joseph Sullivan, Thomas Kelly, and Philip Levy. Described by Burgess as his band of 'merry men'.

There's nothing merry about what they've done.

Henry sketched men lifting rocks to uncover the battered body of gold miner James De Pontius of New York. He was lying face down, his hat next to his head. Henry shuddered as he remembered watching Kelly and Burgess piling rocks on the dead man.

He sketched a police constable as he discovered the body of Felix Mathieu, the Frenchman who used to run the Café de Paris pub at Deep Creek. He was lying on his back, mouth open.

He sketched John Kempthorne, crumpled, shot through the head.

And James Dudley, face to the ground, a handkerchief around his neck. Strangled.

The bodies were deep in the bush, and the gang had not bothered to bury them. They had piled rocks on De Pontius's body and only thrown branches across the others.

Henry stopped sketching and looked away. *I was crazy ever to think of joining Burgess's gang.*

He watched a procession of men, as if in slow-motion, carrying bodies down the mountain track through the mist and rain. The bodies were cradled in canvas hammocks, slung on poles. All victims of Burgess's merry men.

Why am I crying?

Henry's tears mingled with the rain as he listened to the sloshing of the searchers' boots on the rain-soaked mountain path, and the creak of the poles as they strained under the weight of the bodies.

He sketched a procession of men carrying bodies down the mountain track through the mist and rain.

By the time the grim funeral procession reached Nelson, there were some eighty men marching in the torrential rain. At the head of the procession was Sergeant Major Robert Shallcrass, in charge of the police in the district.

When they reached the road, they laid the bodies on horse-drawn drays and carted them to a makeshift morgue in the Nelson Fire Brigade engine house.

Then Henry stood in the crowd as the volunteers marched up Trafalgar Street to the Trafalgar Hotel to report to the search committee. The marchers were sombre because of the grim nature of their task, but elated to have found the missing men. Along the way they were cheered by crowds of locals.

Next day, the *Nelson Express* informed anyone who had not heard the news:

BODIES OF MISSING MEN FOUND ON MAUNGATAPU MOUNTAIN.

What happened next would always baffle Henry.

If he had been in Burgess's gang – *God forbid* – he would have got as far away as possible. *And as fast as possible.* Instead, Burgess and his accomplices stayed right there in town. They went shopping. They drank in bars. They wandered around town and talked to people.

In short, they were far from invisible in Nelson.

And so it was that Henry Appleton found himself leaning against the side of a wooden building with his artist's sketchbook.

He completed a sketch of Richard Burgess – *my father?* – being arrested by Constable Bartholomew Murphy as he walked along Bridge Street.

Did Burgess really think he would go unnoticed in this small town?

Henry avoided Burgess's dark eyes as he was led past by the constable. *I don't want to go near him. He scares me.*

Henry could not put the events of the past few weeks out of his mind. He shuddered when he remembered his treatment at the hands of Burgess and Sullivan. The pain as Kelly's rock struck his leg. And the screams of the murdered men in the hills.

Despite all these ugly memories, he was determined to sketch the next stage of his nightmarish adventures: the arrests of the villains.

So, sketchbook in hand, he went along with the police to the Wakatū Hotel and watched as they arrested Levy. He was sipping a beer and did not put up a struggle. Later, Henry was with the police when they stopped Kelly as he came out of the dining room at the Lord Nelson Hotel. *He's bought himself another fancy waistcoat with money from the murdered travellers.* Henry saw that the loudmouthed Kelly, the man who had sniggered as he carved his own name into the physician's rifle, was now a whimpering prisoner.

And then Sullivan.

This time, Henry stood in the background with his sketchbook. He had no desire to confront this violent man. He watched as constables entered the Mitre Hotel and found Sullivan sitting with a glass of wine.

The whole gang locked up! After all the terrible things they did on Maungatapu Mountain… it's over. They're not so tough now.

He stepped back into the shadows as they brought Sullivan out in handcuffs. The big man, with his mouth a crack in the rock of his face, and his fists clenched tight. *He still gives me the shivers.*

THIRTY-TWO
CONFESSIONS

EVEN IN 1866, AS WELL AS NUMEROUS CHURCHES AND drinking establishments, Nelson had a large and well-built jail – a long, low wooden structure. This was where Burgess was being kept as he awaited trial, and where Henry was about to renew contact with his "father".

Henry arrived at the prison gate carrying a bulky plate camera as Miriama struggled with a heavy tripod.

Henry was now employed at the *Nelson Gazette* – one of three newspapers in this bustling township. Officers of the court had requested photographs of the arrested men, and Burgess insisted it should be Henry who took the pictures.

Henry was excited, but nervous about meeting Burgess again. *I will just take his photo and leave.*

"Are you still willing to do this?" he asked Miriama.

"Of course," she said. "I want to meet this man who might be your father."

"Aren't you … frightened?"

"Of course not. He's locked up, under guard." She

looked at Henry's furrowed brow and smiled. "Henry, how sweet. You're concerned for my wellbeing."

"Well, yes, I am," Henry spluttered. "I – I care about you." He looked away, then back. "A lot."

"And I care for you, Henry," Miriama responded.

Henry reached for her hand, but she pulled back and shook her head. The awkward silence that followed was broken by Sergeant Nash's arrival.

"We've found a good place," he said.

"With plenty of light?" asked Henry.

"You'll see," said the sergeant. He took Henry and Miriama down the prison corridor and into a bare storeroom that led onto the courtyard.

The room faced away from the morning sun, and would provide the even, natural light needed for the photograph.

"Excellent," said Henry.

He and Miriama said nothing more as they set up the tripod and camera. They placed a stool a short distance out from the wall, and Miriama sat on it while Henry checked the position of the camera.

"That will –" said Henry. He coughed to clear his throat. "That will work." He fidgeted with the camera.

"Ready?"

Henry jumped as a voice boomed from the corridor.

It was the burly warder, Frank Jolly. "Burgess is waitin' for ya," he growled. He pointed down the corridor with his night stick. "Thataway."

He followed them, carrying a jacket and waistcoat. "You'll find him a very disagreeable character," Jolly warned them. "My boy Tommy has nightmares about 'im."

When they reached Burgess's cell, he was in leg irons, kneeling in prayer with the Reverend Hadfield. His eyes were closed, and he prayed with gusto. "I am now convinced, O Lord, of thy judgement respectin' me, in havin' broken thy holy laws."

Burgess had embraced Christianity with enthusiasm since being locked up, but only a few people believed he was genuinely remorseful, and Warder Jolly was not one of them. He turned to Henry with a sneer.

"He should o' been on the stage," he said.

Burgess opened one eye and nodded at Henry.

"For thou hast repeatedly said…" Burgess paused, and then proclaimed, along with the Reverend Hadfield, "Judgement is mine. Amen."

Burgess greeted Henry with a wide grin. " 'Enry, fank you for comin'!" The leg irons clattered as he stood. "Come in, come in!"

Has Burgess really changed? Henry wondered. *He seems so – friendly.*

Warder Jolly unlocked the cell. "Dunno why you're doin' this, young man," he said to Henry. "This is the most hated man in the country – and for good reason. Nelson is a place of industrious and honest citizens."

Jolly might just have been quoting the editorial in the *Gazette*, but there was no doubt he reflected the views of the town. Details of the Maungatapu murders horrified people.

Of course, they were also morbidly fascinated by the evil in their midst. Groups of giggling young people had trekked up into the hills to visit what had become known as Murderers' Rock.

Warder Jolly entered the cell and prodded Burgess with his nightstick. "Back to the wall, maggot."

The Reverend Hadfield was happy to slip out of the cell.

"Fank you Reverend," said the outlaw.

So polite!

" 'Enry, lad," said Burgess, "I'm sorry for 'ow Sullivan shot you an' all."

Warder Jolly snorted. "You'll hang for it soon enough."

Burgess ignored him. "I'm gunna set the record straight, 'Enry."

He indicated the small desk and stack of papers in the corner of the cell. "These last weeks I bin writin' a full and frank confession. Everyfink what happened."

Henry was taken aback. "A confession?"

"I know I'm going to 'ang for me black deeds, and quite right too. But I'm not gunna let that slimy rat..." Burgess raised his voice. "...that slimy rat Sullivan get off scot-free."

From down the corridor, a voice roared back in defiance. "You're the murderer, Burgess!"

Sullivan! Henry shivered at the sound of that voice.

"He told the police he was just a lookout," said Henry. *Will anyone believe him?*

Burgess dropped his calm demeanour, and his eyes blazed. "A lookout? Sullivan's a monster," he snarled. "Ready to shed any amount of blood. He was there, I tell ya. Well, you know that, 'Enry."

I do. He almost shed MY blood.

Burgess picked up a sheaf of handwritten notes from the desk. "Listen to this. Me own words. 'We took Dudley about sixty yards from the range and caused 'im to sit on the ground. Then Sullivan…' " he looked up at Henry meaningfully " '…then *Sullivan* took off his sash and put it around his neck. Then, the handkerchief being around his eyes… we strangled him.' "

Warder Jolly grunted. "See what I mean?"

Henry shuddered at the mental picture. *Burgess is writing it all down as if he's proud of it.*

"Sullivan's gunna try an' pin it all on the rest of us," said Burgess. "Me. Kelly. Levy. That's his plan. Dia-bloody-bolical!"

Warder Jolly whacked him across the arm with his nightstick. It was a hefty blow, but Burgess just hissed.

Henry cried out, "Don't!"

Burgess was calm. "It's all right 'Enry. He don't know no better. An' I've seen worse."

He pointed at a sheet of paper stuck to the wall. On it there was a detailed line drawing of a sailing ship, the *President*. There were masts but no sails: this was a convict ship, or "hulk", converted to a floating prison when Melbourne's goals became overcrowded.

"Dozens of us was locked up in irons below deck, for days … weeks … monfs," said Burgess.

"They was floatin' hells of misery. Dark. Filthy. The men were so sick an' 'ungry they looked like walkin' spectres of some uvver world." He paused. "There was times I wished the ship would go to the bottom, and me wiv it."

He grinned at the horrified looks on the faces of Henry and Miriama.

"You sweet young fings don't know nuffink 'bout what they dealt out in them prisons. Look 'ere."

Burgess turned to the wall and lifted his shirt over his head.

Even Warder Jolly was affected by what he saw. "Bloody oath!" he gasped.

THIRTY-THREE
THE PRISONER

Warder Jolly, Henry, and Miriama stared in horror at Burgess's bare back. It was crisscrossed with raised scars and red welts.

"One 'undred lashes one time," Burgess told them. "Gawd that stung!"

Henry had heard about prisoners being whipped as a punishment. Each stroke would bleed. Then another stroke would land on top of the raw flesh. And another. And another. But he had never seen the results on a man's back. *I feel sick. How can men be so cruel?*

Burgess lowered his shirt and faced them again. "Half of them lashes was well deserved. I done some bad stuff. But the uvvers…" His voice cracked, and he shook his head.

WHACK!

In his head Henry heard it clearly: the sickening sound of rope on flesh.

"It were just three years ago," Burgess went on. "Sydney Jail."

Henry shut his eyes and imagined himself in the cold

stone courtyard of an Australian prison.

"They tie yer up, good 'n' tight," said Burgess, "arms outstretched. Shove a stick between ya teeth, so's ya don't bite ya tongue… put a black 'ood over yer 'ead …"

Warder Jolly booted the wall of the cell. "We don't need to hear all this, Burgess."

"Yes, ya bloody do," said Burgess. "These young 'uns need to hear what's done in the name of law an' justice."

Jolly turned away and muttered, and Burgess continued his story.

"Then they wheel out this disgustin' creature called a trusty – one of us, who's sold out to the management for a few extra favours…"

He spat on the floor, and Henry put a protective arm around Miriama.

"An' this trusty, this scum, 'e picks up 'is cat-o'-nine-tails, 'is weapon… an'—

"Whack!"

Henry and Miriam jumped.

"… an' *whack* again!"

Henry and Miriama flinched again. Warder Jolly let out a rumbling growl from deep in his throat.

"The rope opens up ya flesh," said Burgess. "Rope on bloody flesh, again and again. *Whack, whack, whack…*"

"Enough!" cried Jolly. He prodded Burgess in the chest with his stick, making him stumble back against the wall.

"The commandant loved it," said Burgess. " 'e would stand right there, watchin' us poor creatures getting' beat. What a sick worm 'e was."

Burgess looked directly at Warder Jolly.

"I'll tell yer somefin' for nuffink," he said. "I met more

sadistic bastards in uniform than I ever met in prison garb."

Warder Jolly squirmed.

"Me life's been a rough one," said Burgess. "I was treated worse than a mongrel cur of a dog. I swore by 'eaven above to take a 'uman life for every lash and indignity laid on me by the dogs who flogged me."

Henry gulped. One life for every lash! *How many lives did he take?* Some people in town claimed the gang had killed twenty or thirty men during their travels around New Zealand.

Burgess picked up one of the pages he had been writing and half-recited, half-sang the words:

"Before you start to criticise, take a look and you will see,

"I'm a social end product, so don't blame me.

"I'm a social end product: blame society.

"I didn't need to end up like this, 'Enry, but the way I was treated in them prisons… I swore to take me revenge."

No one spoke as they absorbed these chilling words. Then Miriama stepped forward, took the necktie from the warder, and put it around Burgess's collar.

Their eyes met, hers pure, his disturbed.

"Every soul is a soul worth saving," she whispered.

Burgess shot back, "The devil 'as mine."

"You can get it back," said Miriama. Quietly, she put a folded note in his hand. "It's never too late."

Burgess glanced at the note, then tucked it under his blanket. Now he was cheery again. "Get on wiv it, 'Enry! Take me picher."

Warder Jolly herded Burgess out of his cell, his leg chains echoing harshly down the corridor.

"I'm a free man, Sullivan!" Burgess yelled gleefully, in the direction of his accomplice's cell.

"That'll be the day!" roared Sullivan.

Warder Jolly prodded Burgess with his stick. "Enough, Burgess." He bundled him into the storeroom where Henry had set up his camera.

Burgess took his waistcoat and jacket from Warder Jolly, put them on, and climbed onto the stool. He winked at Henry. "This picher'll make yer famous, son, after the trial."

Henry took refuge beneath the black cloth behind the camera and framed his shot. *He's so confident. As if he's done something to be proud of!*

"Would you straighten your necktie please, Mister Burgess?"

"*Mister* Burgess?" snorted Jolly. "Sonny, this low life don't deserve no 'mister'."

Henry avoided looking into Burgess's steely eyes. *Such scary eyes!* They were sometimes hazel and sometimes seemed black. He studied him through the lens. *Is this how history will remember Burgess the murderer?*

Burgess sat straight, one hand on his hip. Only the top button of his jacket was done up, in the fashion of the day.

He looks just like a businessman, mused Henry. *You can't tell a man's character from his appearance.*

He focused the shot. "Hold very still, Mister Burgess."

Henry reached around and removed the lens cap. "Very still…" He counted to five and replaced the cap. "Thank you, sir."

It was over.

Miriama removed the photographic plate holder and hurried off to develop the negative.

"Git them good clothes off," ordered Jolly. He waited for Burgess to remove the jacket and waistcoat, then prodded him back towards his cell.

Henry took a deep breath, and was beginning to pack away his camera gear when he realised someone was standing outside the door.

"Doctor Smith!"

"Henry," Smith greeted him in a brittle voice.

Henry saw Smith was holding the boxes that contained his fingerprinting gear. Before he could ask, the doctor headed down the corridor. He heard Burgess's chains rattle.

"Ah, the good doctor," Burgess chortled. "He reckons he's gunna prove I killed his missus. Ain't that right, Doc?"

Henry crept into the corridor and stood next to Sergeant Nash at the door to Burgess's cell. They watched as Smith set up his fingerprinting gear.

Warder Jolly stood next to Burgess, his stick at the ready. Henry was surprised to see the doctor's hands were trembling.

"No need to be scared o' me, Doc," said Burgess. "I ain't got no beef wiv you."

"I'm not scared of you, Burgess," Smith fired back. "I simply find it hard to be steady in the presence of the insect that killed my wife."

"I ain't done no such fing!" Burgess protested.

"I believe you have – you did," the doctor responded. "And I can prove it."

Burgess looked closely at Smith, and asked, "Have our paths crossed before, guvnor?"

"Yes. When you sliced my throat." Smith lowered his scarf to show the scar on his neck.

"Bah! That don't look like my 'andiwork," said Burgess. "And anyway, I never killed yer missus."

Henry came closer to listen.

"I 'ave indeed finished awf a few gentlemen down the years," said Burgess. "But I never done no 'arm to no lady." His leg chains rattled as he spread his arms, Christ-like, as if to proclaim his innocence.

Henry could imagine Burgess doing the same in the Australian desert – a mad man dancing around a campfire, arms outstretched, spinning and firing his pistol in the air.

Suddenly Burgess was quieter. "Makes me fink of Carrie," he said.

Carrie? Henry was curious. He had never heard this name before.

"Me missus."

Everyone in the cell fell silent.

"I intended for 'er to share me bread for the remainder of me days. But I left 'er in 'Okitika." Burgess lowered his eyes. "She was wiv child, too."

Henry recalled Burgess's own story: how his father in England had abandoned him. This seemed to set the course for his life. *Now Burgess has done the same!* Henry wondered what would happen to Carrie and her baby. Burgess's baby.

Burgess looked directly at Smith, and repeated, "I never 'armed no lady." He held out his hand. "Take me print."

Smith rolled back Burgess's sleeve. Then he stopped, frowning.

"Australia. Carbolic acid!" He stared at Burgess. "It was you!"

"Whaa?" Burgess looked blank. But Henry remembered: the grim story that Doctor Smith had recounted in the sergeant's office. How he had treated an injured man who asked about carbolic acid, and how he removed a bullet from the man's shoulder…

Clearly Smith had recognized that man as Burgess. But he said nothing more, and set about taking a print of Burgess's thumb. He placed a piece of clean paper on a small box, to enable Burgess to place his thumb horizontally.

Warder Jolly, Sergeant Nash, and Henry crowded around him, keen to see this new science in action. Smith gripped Burgess's hand and rolled his thumb onto the paper from one side to the other. This left a clean image of his thumb, complete with its complex pattern of lines.

Burgess whistled. "Bloody 'mazing!"

With great care, Smith took out the thumbprint of his wife's killer: the precious clue he had carried with him on his long quest. Under a magnifying glass, he compared the two prints.

"This gadget would've been bloody useful back in London," Burgess whispered to Henry. "I were framed for somefink I never done. I were just walkin' down the road, innocent like, when –"

Clatter! The magnifier hit the floor, and Smith sank to his knees.

Henry stared at him. *What's happened?*

Smith was shaking again.

Do the prints match? Did Burgess kill the doctor's wife?

Sergeant Nash touched Smith's shoulder. "Doctor Smith?"

Smith looked up at the sergeant, his face white. "It's not him," he said.

THIRTY-FOUR

COLD-BLOODED MURDER

"THIS IS NOT THE MAN WHO MURDERED MY WIFE," DOCTOR Smith pronounced with certainty, his voice shaky.

So Burgess was telling the truth!

Burgess whooped. "I bloody told ya!"

The sergeant took a look for himself. He could see at a glance that the thumb prints were very, very different. "Well, that's a turn-up for the books," he said.

Burgess crowed. "I told ya, I never done 'arm no lady!"

Smith slumped forward and buried his head in his hands.

"Anyhow," Burgess chortled, "whatcha plannin' to do when you find the bugger what *actually* killed yer missus? Eh?"

In a daze, Smith got to his feet.

Burgess kept pushing. "Youse gunna cook him, ain't ya?!" He mimicked strangulation.

Smith rounded on him. "A man must pay for the evil he does."

Burgess shook his head. "Wiv due respeck, Doc – the Bible says 'Judge not, saith the Lord'."

Henry stared in wonder at Burgess: a multiple murderer quoting from the Bible.

"It'll be the good Lord what decides who's gunna pay," Burgess told Smith. "You bloody nearly killed the wrong man!"

Yes, he did!

Smith packed up his fingerprinting gear and headed for the door.

Burgess called after him. "You and I are two peas in a pod, Doc."

Smith halted. "What?!"

"Peas in a pod," Burgess repeated. "You and me – we both got our 'reasons' for murder. Mine's gold. Yours be 'revenge'. Still murder in my book."

I tried to tell the doctor that.

Henry hobbled off down the corridor, keen to get out of this grim place. But Burgess hadn't finished. His cry echoed after them down the hall.

"Ya know it was Sullivan wot killed ya missus, don'tcha."

Smith stopped. "Sullivan?"

Henry heard the eerie cracking of the big man's knuckles.

"Sullivan's yer man for sure," called Burgess.

Smith turned to the sergeant. "Sergeant, let me fingerprint Sullivan." He made a dash for the corridor, but Nash restrained him.

"Doctor Smith, I'm sorry, but I cannot let you disrupt proceedings further."

Smith continued to push against Nash. "Sergeant, I beg you…"

"Why, Doctor? All of these men are about to be tried for murder anyway – and they're bound to hang."

"It will take but a few minutes," said Smith, "to set my mind at rest."

The sergeant tugged at his moustache and studied the man in front of him, his bloodshot eyes pleading. "Very well," he said. "But only if Sullivan agrees. I'm not going to hold the man down in order to get his fingerprints."

"Thank you, Sergeant," cried Smith. He pushed forward, restrained by the policeman, until he was at the door of Sullivan's cell.

"Sullivan!" the sergeant barked.

The prisoner was against the far wall, largely hidden in the shadows. He said nothing. Henry ventured closer to watch.

"Sullivan," the sergeant continued. "You heard all that. Are you willing to have your fingerprints taken?"

No response.

"To prove you are not the man who killed Doctor Smith's wife?"

No response.

"Sullivan – will you?" Smith called out in a broken voice.

A growl came from inside the dark cell. "Eat me boots," said the voice.

Smith pressed against the cell door. "You can prove your innocence," he pleaded.

"I don't owe you nuffink," Sullivan bellowed.

From the cell down the corridor came Burgess's cry: " 'E's the one! Take 'is prints!"

"You're the monster, Burgess!" Sullivan yelled back.

The sergeant pulled Smith away from the door. "Enough," he said. "He's not going to give way, and I am not going to send in the troops to force him."

Smith's shoulders dropped. He let out a deep sigh and allowed himself to be shepherded out of the prison.

Burgess yelled after him, his voice echoing down the corridor. "Pray for me darkened soul!"

Henry lingered, and watched Burgess reach under his pillow and picked up a piece of paper. He stood, engrossed, and read it through. He pondered the message, then read it again. "Sweet soul," he whispered.

Henry hurried off towards the main doors. He would come back later for his camera. Right now, he wanted to talk to Doctor Smith.

He found him outside the prison gate. He was leaning against a post, biting his lip and scuffing his boots in the dirt.

"Sullivan," he said. "All this time it was Sullivan I should have been pursuing."

Henry nodded, remembering his own terrifying encounters with the rock-faced man with the big boots and the big knife. "He's the worst of them all." *Yes, he was going to kill me.*

"The sergeant reckons they'll all hang," said Smith. He sounded uncertain.

"That's what you want, isn't it, sir?"

"I would prefer to do the task myself." Smith stooped and pulled from his boot a length of cord. Henry gasped.

"What is that?"

"A garotte," said Smith. He put a hand around his throat and squeezed. "I was ready to dispatch him there and then."

"That'd be cold-blooded murder!"

"Do you think so, Henry? If the law sends an evil man to the gallows, it's 'justice', but if an individual does the same, it's 'murder'?"

He marched off. Henry watched. *Until now, I idolised you…*

Henry looked up at the cold walls of the prison. Inside was Burgess, a murderer, about to hang. And out here, walking free – Doctor Smith, planning his own private execution.

While Henry was pondering this, Smith turned around with an announcement. "I'm going back to Australia, Henry."

"What about the trial?"

"I cannot sit in court and listen to those weasels trying to justify what they've done," said Smith. He held out his hand. "There's a boat leaving for Sydney tonight."

Henry was barely aware of Smith shaking his hand.

"You're a good man, Henry. You'll make a fine doctor."

Henry frowned. *How can I become a doctor?*

Smith put a hand on Henry's shoulder.

"I will send you money for your training, Henry. To become a physician. Like I used to be." *Used to be?*

"Humanity needs people like you, Henry. People with compassion." His eyes dropped. "God knows I no longer have any."

Henry watched him walk away.

Strangely, in all this time, he had not thought about Miriama. But he did now. He called after Smith. "What about Miriama?"

THIRTY-FIVE
MIRIAMA'S DECISION

THE DOCTOR TURNED AND OFFERED HENRY A SMALL SHRUG, then walked off.

I can't lose Miriama too!

Henry became aware of a heartless chuckle behind him. He turned. Chadwick and his friend Arthur Luxton were sniggering.

"Why are you here, Mister Chadwick?" demanded Henry.

"We're here to visit your unsavoury friend Burgess," said Chadwick.

Chadwick and Luxton were both known in town as phrenologists, and Henry knew they were keen to study Burgess. Chadwick pulled out a measuring tape, and had wrapped it around Henry's head before he could move away.

"We will be measuring Burgess's skull to see exactly what dark deeds the man is capable of."

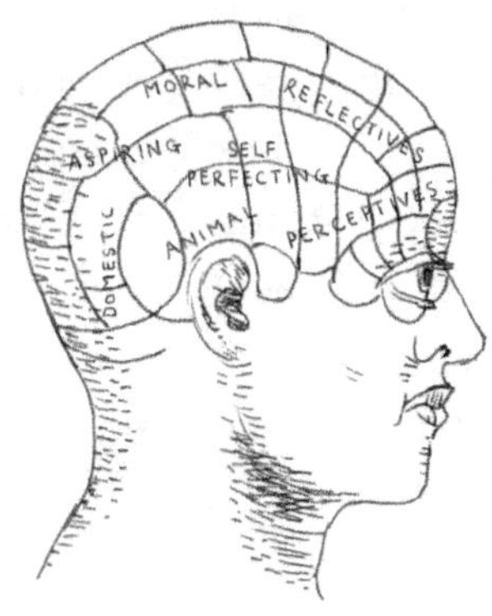

"We will be measuring Burgess's skull," said
Chadwick, "to see exactly what dark deeds the man is
capable of."

Henry ripped away the measuring tape. "You can't do that!"

"Oh yes, we can. We have permission. And Burgess's agreement."

Luxton held up his chart showing the drawing of a man's skull. It was divided into many segments, marked with words like "Destructiveness", "Veneration", "Self-Perfecting", "Intellect", "Combativeness", "Acquisitiveness".

"Your friend Burgess is a captain over devils," said Chadwick.

Henry watched as Chadwick and Luxton were escorted into the prison and disappeared down the corridor towards the cells.

Then he remembered. "Miriama!" *She's going to leave me.* He stumbled away, unsteady on his walking stick.

A poem pushed itself into his head.

"Picture me dead on the wall—

"Would that fill your heart with sorrow?"

It was not one of the great Victorian poems, certainly, but it was one he wrote himself, a few weeks ago in the depths of self-pity, and he could not get it out of his mind.

"Falling from Nelson Town Hall—

"Would you want to follow?"

Henry surveyed the prison. Horses. Passers-by. Then he snapped out of his daydream.

I must find her.

He ran – hobbled – down a side road.

Miriama, where are you?

He reached the main street; the poem playing on in his head:

"I don't really know, but I don't think so—

"For you don't love me that well."

He hobbled around the side of the hotel to the stables.

There she is!

He watched from the door as Miriama talked to her horse, stroking its jaw.

"Miriama!" he called out in a croaky voice.

She looked up and smiled. But it was not a happy smile.

"Miriama, please don't go!" Henry blurted out. "I... I..."

I love you, Miriama. Could he say it out loud? He took a step towards her.

"I love you!"

The words emerged in a squeaky voice that made Henry cringe, so he said it again in a deeper voice. "I love you."

Miriama had been crying. She moved close to him and touched his hand. "I must go with Doctor Smith. We have an agreement."

An agreement? What about us?

"He wants me to work with him a while longer."

Henry put his hand on top of hers. "Don't go!" he pleaded.

Miriama looked deeply into his eyes. "It won't be forever, Henry."

She placed her lips lightly on his cheek.

Henry had never been kissed by anyone other than his mother, and Miriama's kiss took his breath away. He was still breathless as she turned and hurried from the stables.

Henry swayed, then stumbled out to watch her enter the hotel. He retreated into the alley and slumped to the ground. Lonely and lovesick, in an empty lane.

He whacked his walking stick against the wall, and in his head he taunted himself with the last line of his poem.

"No, you don't love me that well."

It was a line that would stay in Henry's mind over the next few months, as he pined for his missing friends and struggled to lead a normal life.

Spring arrived, but it did not bring a fresh start or new hope for Henry. Although his injured leg was healing, the doctors said he would always need a walking stick.

A walking stick, like an old man. Forever!

The walking stick would be an everlasting reminder of his ordeal at the hands of the Burgess gang.

THIRTY-SIX
THE TRIAL

Henry's mother reached under the bed for the shiny boots once worn by her husband, William Henry Appleton. She dusted them with gentle sweeps of a well-worn cloth, then carried them into the kitchen where Henry was waiting. She presented the boots to him on her open palms, almost as if this was a religious ceremony.

His mother was solemn, but Henry could not help grinning as he accepted the precious boots. He had waited a long time for this moment. He pulled off his old boots and showed his mother the holes in the soles. Then he pulled on his father's boots and laced them up.

"Perfect," said his mother softly.

As Henry stood to hug her, his eyes fell on William Appleton's stopwatch on the wall. He waited as his mother held the timepiece and wound it. Then she blinked a tear from her eye and gave Henry a determined smile.

"Time to go," she said.

It was Wednesday, September 12, 1866. The trial of the Burgess gang was scheduled to begin this day.

Henry hitched Duke to an open buggy to take them to the courthouse.

For the first time in months they had dressed in formal attire: Henry in his father's suit, threadbare but recognisably well-tailored, and his mother in the long blue dress with lace and velvet trimmings she had worn as an English lady back in London.

She had chosen this dress when she had said goodbye to friends and family she knew she would never see again. Never.

Henry wondered if she was thinking of them now, as they trotted past the clusters of daffodils which swayed in the breeze alongside the dirt road.

Henry had the reins while his mother read aloud from a letter they had received the previous day. It was from Miriama, who was still in Australia.

His mother looked up from the letter. "She says she's horrified by the conditions of the aboriginal people in Australia. But she feels the same way in New Zealand."

She read: "I am landless and powerless in my own country."

She folded the letter away.

"Nothing personal?" asked Henry, frowning. *Nothing about me? After all we've been through?*

"No, just news," she replied. She saw the look on her son's face and added, "Miriama will come back to New Zealand one day, Henry, I'm sure. This is where she belongs."

"This is where I belong, too, Mother." He pursed his lips. "I know you want to go back to England. But this is my home now."

"Even if we lose the farm?"

Henry grunted.

"Let's wait till after the trial," said his mother.

Henry grimaced.

————

The stately Nelson Provincial Hall had been refitted as a courtroom to accommodate the large numbers of people expected. Henry pulled up next to a dozen other horses and carts.

At the doors, crowds of men and women were milling around, chattering loudly. Henry hitched the buggy and helped his mother step down. A boy ran up with an armful of news sheets and thrust one in Henry's face. He looked at the heading:

THE MAUNGATAPU MURDERS!!! Vivid details of their crimes and capture! With sketches and maps.

"Disgusting," said Henry's mother. "They're making this into a circus."

But Henry gave the boy a coin – he was earning his own money these days at the *Gazette* – and took a sheet.

He caught a glimpse of a heading – *The Holdup!* Below, a sketch of four highwaymen on a mountain track, next to the Maungatapu rock. They were pointing weapons at travellers with horses.

"I suppose that's the work of your Johnny Slick," his mother sniffed.

Henry wondered too. He stuffed the sheet in his jacket to study later.

They pushed through the crowds, up the steps to the main doors. Henry heard people whispering,

"That's them."

An official waved them through, into the imposing halls with polished wooden floors that echoed every word. Into the packed courtroom.

Henry took it all in, as if in a dream.

There were boos and hisses from the crowd as Burgess, Kelly, and Levy were escorted in. They were handcuffed but wore civilian clothes, and stood in a specially built raised dock, facing the judge.

Henry looked around for Sullivan. *Ah, over there.* The big man was sitting with the police and legal teams and was not wearing handcuffs. *You're the worst of them all, Sullivan, and yet you're a free man because you lied.*

Henry remembered how Sergeant Nash had assured Doctor Smith that all four highwaymen would be put on trial, but it was not to be so. Sullivan had turned "Queen's Evidence", and he would tell the court his version of what happened in the hills, in the hope that the rest of the gang would be found guilty and he would be set free.

The sound of a gavel. Tap tap tap! The court usher called out: "Silence in court!"

Members of the special jury – twelve local men chosen for their "good standing" – included two farmers, a clerk, an accountant, an auctioneer, and three described only as "gentlemen". Their foreman was a prominent farmer and businessman, Mr Charles Canning. They shuffled in their seats, perhaps excited to be minor stars in a "celebrity" trial that everyone in town was talking about.

Henry sat next to his mother. He looked around the public gallery and spotted Chadwick.

All the men from my nightmares are here!

The bank manager smirked. And Richard Burgess, of course. He saw Henry and gave him a cocky smile and a wink.

"Don't look at him, Henry," hissed his mother.

How can I stop? He's a murderer and he says he's my father.

Henry noticed his mother was rubbing her wrists. She always did this when she was anxious. The wounds from the ropes that the Burgess gang used to tie her up had never healed properly.

My mother's wrists… my own broken leg… we're lucky to be alive.

Henry shut his eyes and relived scenes from the past few weeks: his ambush by Burgess, Sullivan's knife, Sullivan's great fists, Burgess's invitation to join his "merry men", the pain as Kelly's rock struck his leg…

The screams of the gold miners… and the bodies in the forest…

Burgess took the stand, and Henry's eyes sprang open.

There he was – *my father?* – standing upright in the dock, head held high as if he were a respected community figure. He was reading from his notes in a clear voice. "The confession of Burgess the Murderer," he began.

There were murmurs of astonishment from the gallery. Henry shook his head. He could hardly believe what he was hearing.

There was Burgess – *my father?* – standing upright in the dock.
"The confession of Burgess the Murderer," he began.

THIRTY-SEVEN
THE VERDICT

Henry knew that Burgess, during his long days in prison, had written a journal describing all his ghastly exploits in horrifying detail. The shootings, robberies, holdups, stabbings, the murders of innocent men – covering the two decades since he had been transported to Australia as a young pickpocket.

But why? Why tell everyone?

Burgess addressed the judge, and a court official wrote down every word. "My motive, sir, is not to amuse. I wish to warn young and foolish people from following my steps."

It amazed Henry to hear Burgess speak this way. Gone was the exaggerated Cockney accent and the frequent use of slang. He was addressing the court in the manner of an educated Englishman.

There were sniggers from the public gallery. The judge raised his eyebrows.

"Indeed, Mister Burgess?"

Burgess continued.

"Another motive, sir, equally important – is that your penal code, your rigid enforcement of strict discipline, never does any good."

The judge bristled.

He's right, thought Henry. *I've seen what they did to him in prison.*

"In fact," said Burgess, "your prisons and solitary confinements become places where new crimes are hatched. Thus society is preyed on by men who are educated to do evil while undergoing punishment."

Henry marvelled at how articulate this highwayman was. Burgess had left school early – expelled, most likely – and yet at times spoke like the most well-read of men. Not that his critique of the penal system found any support. There was a mumble of conversation among the courtroom crowd.

Henry glanced at Chadwick and was rewarded with a sneer.

The judge rapped his gavel. "Silence!"

Burgess shuffled his papers, then read loud and clear, his voice able to be heard in every corner of the courtroom and down the corridors.

"Written in my dungeon drear, in the year of Grace 1866…"

He's clever. But evil.

Burgess marched on with his horrifying narrative. He was allowed to read out his entire story, which took him a full five hours.

Henry could see that Burgess was enjoying the limelight. He was a Shakespearean actor on the stage, delivering the performance of his life, with an attentive audience packing the theatre. He knew the impact of his grisly accounts, and often looked up from his papers, pausing for effect, before addressing the public gallery.

"And then," he read, "we strangled him."

Henry's mother gasped in horror, along with many of the spectators.

On and on Burgess rambled, providing all the evidence any jury would need to convict him. Finally, he ended his reading: "I have signed my own death warrant."

You have, Burgess. You certainly have.

Days passed. Burgess and Kelly had addressed the court at length – one acknowledging his crimes, the other protesting his innocence. Levy said little, although he proclaimed he had no part in any murders.

"I am happy to inform you," he told the judge calmly, "that in my own mind, and from the bottom of my heart, by the God I worship, I leave this bar an innocent man."

As for Sullivan, he added damning facts about the Maungatapu murders and a good few lies, all the time maintaining his own innocence.

Then the trial was over.

The jury returned after only fifty-five minutes and announced that they found all three men guilty.

Now the judge was passing sentence. He looked up at the clock, then at Burgess.

Henry's mind was racing – *is this my father?* – and he heard only snippets of the judge's words: "A cruel assassin," he called Burgess. "One of the wickedest of men."

The judge said Burgess was a man "without any kindly feeling for his fellows."

No kindly feeling? Yet Henry knew Burgess always stood up for his mates. *And he protected me from Sullivan.*

The judge leant forward and eyeballed Burgess. He accused him of having "some of the cunning of the fox and a little more than the blood-thirstiness of the wolf."

Blood-thirstiness? Henry could not help but look over at Sullivan at this point. The big man was smirking as the judge heaped those words on Burgess.

You are just as blood-thirsty, Sullivan.

Henry's gaze remained focused on Sullivan. He knew the big man had claimed a reward for providing details of the gang's activities and had put all the blame on Burgess. He looked at Sullivan's huge hands as they gripped the wooden bench where he sat.

Those hands!

Henry recalled Doctor Smith's description of the murder of his wife, Alicia in Australia. In his mind's eye, Henry saw her lying on the floor in a pool of blood. He saw big hands pull back Smith's head and bring a knife to his throat. He saw the face of the intruder as he steadied himself against a chest of drawers. The face was Sullivan's.

Henry opened his eyes to see the judge placing a cap of black silk on his head.

Burgess was silent, but Kelly waved his arms in desperation. "God forbid!" he screamed. "God forgive you!"

Men and women in the courtroom watched wide-eyed as Kelly shouted and kicked the dock.

"Silence!" The judge rapped his gavel. Then, with black silk on his head, he pronounced the sentence of death for all three accused men:

"… that you be hanged by the neck until your body be dead."

Burgess and Levy stood erect, grim. But Kelly had to be held up by guards.

The judge concluded: "…and may Almighty God have mercy on your souls".

Burgess bowed his head. In a steady voice he addressed the judge. "Your Honour, I have deserved my sentence, and I receive it with humility."

Is he crying? Henry leant forward to study Burgess's face. *Yes, he's crying!*

"He's crying for himself, not his victims," said Henry's mother.

Henry was not so sure. But there was no doubt Burgess was enjoying the attention. He watched as reporters hurried out to file their stories.

Next day, the broadsheets would tell their hungry readers:

BRUTAL HIGHWAYMEN FOUND GUILTY.
BURGESS AND GANG TO MEET THE GALLOWS.

Henry shuddered. He looked at Sullivan. *You deserve to hang too!*

Sullivan was still smirking when the sergeant snapped handcuffs on him. Sullivan looked bewildered. Henry was surprised too – but he watched with satisfaction.

Sergeant John Nash told Sullivan, loud enough for the spectators to hear, "Joseph Sullivan, you are to be put on trial for the murder of Jamie Battle."

Of course! Sullivan's pardon had covered the murder of

the four travellers from Canvas Town, but not the murder of the old flax-cutter.

They can still put him on trial for that crime.

Henry remembered the scruffy old man on the Maungatapu track, telling Sullivan he had just been cutting flax. He remembered the screams as Burgess and Sullivan dragged him into the bushes. And he remembered the thump of Sullivan's fist on Jamie Battle's frail chest.

Henry watched Sullivan being led away. He vowed not go to Sullivan's trial, and he hoped never to see the big man again.

THIRTY-EIGHT
LETTER TO MIRIAMA

As Henry stood, about to leave the court, there was a scream. Henry looked up to see Sullivan tear off his handcuffs and throw Sergeant Nash to the ground. He swung around to face Henry, and called out, "Now you're gonna pay, you little worm!"

The big man hurdled the courtroom benches, charging towards Henry. He sent chairs flying. From nowhere, he produced a butcher's knife. "I'm gonna cut out your heart!"

Henry couldn't move. He watched in slow-motion horror as Sullivan crashed towards him, and he prepared to feel the slice of the cold blade.

"Help me!" he screamed.

"Henry!" his mother shouted. "Henry, wake up!"

Henry sat bolt upright in bed. His mother was shaking his shoulders. His bedclothes were in a tangle.

"Sullivan!" Henry panted.

His mother smiled. "It's all over, Henry. We'll never see Sullivan again."

Henry watched in slow-motion horror as the big
man crashed towards him.

Henry wiped his brow. *Maybe. But he'll always be in my nightmares.* Trembling from the terror of his dream, Henry dressed and sat down to write a letter to Miriama.

He would tell her about the conclusion of the trial, and the fate of the three highwaymen. He would enjoy telling her that Sullivan had been found guilty of Jamie Battle's murder and sent to prison.

How do I start?

"My dear Miriama," he said under his breath. He was

not used to writing letters, and it helped to say the words out loud before committing them to paper.

He tried it another way. "Dearest Miriama," he said, and he dashed it down on paper before he could change his mind.

Henry considered providing some grisly details about Burgess's crimes. He knew Miriama thought there was "some good" in Burgess. Perhaps informing her how brutal the man was would make her see she was wrong. But he decided against it.

He had nearly filled the page with news before he managed to say what was most important to him. He wrote: *I love you, Miriama, and hope that very soon you will return.*

He signed his name carefully at the bottom of the page: *Your Friend, Henry Appleton.*

Henry Appleton. Not Henry Burgess. *Imagine if I had never been adopted. I might be living in a London slum, signing my name Henry Burgess!*

He placed the letter in an envelope, and called to his mother, who was toiling in the garden. "I'm off to town to mail this letter."

That's not exactly true, he rebuked himself. *I'm also going to see Richard Burgess.*

It was Friday, October 5, 1866. The hanging was scheduled for 8 am.

The condemned man had sent for him.

What does he want?

Henry waved to his mother. *She knows where I'm going. But she'll understand – it's my last chance to see my father. The man who might be my father. Is he?*

The dawn light had barely crept across the yard when Henry mounted Duke and galloped off towards Nelson. He took the familiar route past Maungatapu Rock – Murderers' Rock, they were calling it these days – and then through the forest, past the graveyard and chapel. Although many months had gone by since his harrowing adventures in the forest, Henry still shuddered as he took this path.

As he approached the prison, he saw a crowd had already gathered outside. Dozens of Nelson Militia Volunteers had formed a cordon around the walls to keep out over-curious members of the public.

Up on Church Hill, there were knots of people hoping to get a better view. But they could see only the top of the upper beam of the scaffold.

The sounds of sawing and hammering echoed across the open space: normally such innocent noises, but now a chilling reminder that gallows were being readied for a triple hanging.

How barbaric! Do they have to die in such a horrible way?

Duke whinnied, stomped his hooves and flicked his mane. Henry patted his horse's neck. "I know, I know – you don't like crowds, do you boy. Neither do I."

Henry directed his steed away from the prison, to a patch of juicy grass beneath a clump of trees. "How's this, Duke? You'll be happy here."

He tied the reins to a low branch, gave his horse a comforting pat, and strode back around the prison walls. Despite his injured leg and the walking stick, he was determined not to look like an old man.

He saw American dime novel writer Johnny Slick

among the gaggle of newspaper reporters clustered outside the prison gates.

Henry remembered the day, as a nervous would-be writer, he had stumbled into a dim hotel room to meet his hero. Now that man was waiting for *him*.

"Henry!"

"Mister Slick?" Henry had not seen the American for weeks. He assumed he had left the country.

"Henry, I was hopin' to see ya," the dime novelist gushed.

"Why are you here, sir?" *To write about the hanging, obviously. How ghoulish.*

"Ah bin commissioned to take notes on the hangin's. Prisoners' last words, and so on."

Henry grimaced.

"Ah know, ah know," said Slick. "But the readers demand it. Hungry wolves. They devour every darn word."

Henry began to move towards the gates. "I need to go, sir."

But Johnny Slick held him back. "Henry – I must ask." He stared into Henry's eyes. "Allow me the privilege of writing your story."

"*My* story?"

"Yes siree – your part in the whole darn adventure."

Henry looked down at his walking stick. *Adventure? Try nightmare.*

Johnny Slick gave Henry an endearing smile and held out his open palms. "Henry, son – you're a hero. A real live bona fide hero." He pondered his own words. "In fact, one o' the few genuine heroes this old scribe has met!"

Henry shrugged it off. *I used to love your dime novels. Not anymore.*

"Why don't you just make it up, as you usually do?"

"Ouch!" laughed the American. "Ah am stung, Henry. But I sure would value the opportunity to tell the real story. The 'facts', as it were."

Henry studied Johnny Slick – a shambolic, boozy hulk.

"Tell me your story, Henry?"

Henry was not moved. *Three men are about to die, and you just want a "story".*

"Go and see von Tempsky," he said. "He'll give you a good story."

He walked past Slick and up to the gate, where a guard was waiting.

Behind him, Slick sighed and joined reporters from the local newspapers as they were ushered into the prison courtyard, along with official witnesses, half a dozen justices of the peace, and a few government and prison officials.

Their task was to make sure that "justice" was served; to verify that each of the three men was hanged by the neck "until his body be dead".

THIRTY-NINE
THE HANGMAN ARRIVES

As Sergeant Nash escorted Henry along the dark prison corridor, Burgess's Cockney voice rang out.

"Go easy, matey!"

Henry peered through the bars and saw Burgess, still shackled, having his hair hacked off by Warder Jolly. The bushy beard and sideburns had already gone, and he looked a different man.

Hovering nearby, Bible in hand, was the Reverend Hadfield. "Yet shall I fear no evil, for thou art by my side…"

Burgess seemed almost cheerful, and interrupted the minister. "I 'ave no more fear of death than goin' to a weddin'," he declared.

A noise in the courtyard distracted the Reverend Hadfield, and he peered out the window. Henry noted how the shadows of the bars fell across the minister's face, and how he flinched at the sounds of sporadic last-minute hammering.

Warder Jolly finished his work, and Sergeant Nash

unlocked the cell to allow Henry to enter. Burgess stroked his bald scalp.

" 'Enry my boy! Whatcha reckon?" He swivelled his head to show off his haircut.

Henry stared. Most of Burgess's scalp had never seen the sun, and it was so white it glowed, ghost-like in the morning light.

You look scarier than ever. "Mister Burgess – you sent for me?"

Burgess's face darkened. " 'Enry, I only got 'alf an hour left in this world. For the love of God, don't call me 'mister'."

Seeing the change in Burgess's demeanour, Sergeant Nash and Warder Jolly moved closer. Burgess threw up his hands to show he meant no harm, and spoke quietly. " 'Enry, I arksed the good sergeant to fetch youse 'ere cos I 'ave a gift for ya. Made it wiv me own 'ands."

A gift?

Burgess held out a parchment the size of a handkerchief, covered in closely written words.

The handwritten text was arranged in the shape of a crucifix. Surrounding it were drawings of trees, horses and – Henry recognized it at once – the distinctive Maungatapu Rock.

"For old time's sake, 'Enry," said Burgess. He pointed out some of the details. "There's your 'orse – what's 'is name? Duke. There's the eggs what broke. And 'ere's a wee ditty." He tapped at the scrawled words. "I wrote it special for youse."

Henry took the parchment and admired the neatly written text.

Jeepers – this is quite beautiful! It must have taken him ages to write. "Thank you, sir."

"It's a map for yer future," said Burgess.

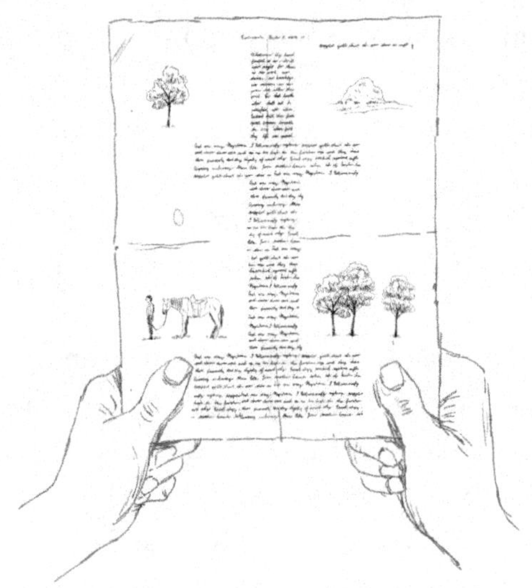

"It's a map for yer future," said Burgess.

"Whatsoever thy hand findeth to do –", Henry began to read aloud. But Burgess interrupted. "Later, son. Later. An' read it careful, mind. It'll lead ya to a treasure ov great worth."

Burgess looked to the minister, then to the heavens. "Amen."

The minister echoed him. "Amen."

The sergeant rattled the keys. "Come on, Burgess. Enough."

Burgess clattered forward in his chains, as if to embrace Henry. Warder Jolly held him back, but Burgess took hold of Henry's shoulders and hissed in his ear. " 'Enry – call me farva."

"I can't." *I don't want you to be my father. I'm not like you.*

Burgess squeezed tighter. "Just once, for pity's sake?"

I can't. Henry broke free and ran for the door.

" 'Enry!" Henry turned and saw Burgess holding out his bony hands to him, his lips trembling, eyes pleading.

I can't!

Henry stumbled into the corridor and heard the clanging of the cell door behind him. Then he detected a new noise. Unfamiliar. A scraping. He looked up to see a black spectre looming at the end of the corridor.

The hangman.

Henry pressed against the wall as the procession came closer. The hangman, wearing a mask of black crepe, approached with two guards. They shuffled past Henry and stopped at the entrance to Burgess's cell.

The angel of death coming to claim his victim! Henry retreated down the corridor.

He emerged from the prison, Burgess's parchment in hand, blinking in the sunlight. Onlookers strained to see past him, into the prison.

An old woman called out, "Did you see them, laddie? The monsters?"

I can't stand this. Vultures circling a dying man.

A hawker shoved a newsprint booklet in his face. Henry couldn't avoid looking at it. There was a sketch he'd seen before, depicting men with rifles peering from behind Maungatapu Rock.

Henry glanced at the heading:

A series of sketches illustrating the principal incidents in connection with the MAUNGATAPU MURDERS.

Henry pushed the hawker aside. *Everyone is trying to make money out of this tragedy.*

The hawker was determined to sell his booklet, and shouted in Henry's face, "All about the trial, guv – sketches, reports, etcetera, etcetera." He flicked open the booklet to show a formal photo of Burgess.

Henry gulped: It was the photo of Burgess he himself had taken in the prison storeroom.

"Look, sir – photographs of the actual killers."

His face – my photo – has become a souvenir. Henry backed away, bumping into the guard at the gate. "May I go back in?" he asked.

The guard was interested only in the crowd swarming around him, and let Henry slip back inside.

"Step away, all of you!" The guard gave the hawker a shove.

The hawker wasn't finished, and yelled at Henry's back. "Only one shilling, sir!"

Henry found himself alone, back in the prison corridor. The shouts and chattering of the crowd became muted, and Henry felt as though he had stepped into another world. He looked around, unsure of what to do. Then he recalled the storeroom where he had taken Burgess's photograph. He hurried to the door and darted inside.

It was dark in here and smelt like an old laundry cupboard. In one corner, a trickle of water ran down the walls.

With a shiver of excitement, Henry realised no one knew

he was here. He was in an ideal position to see and hear everything that was going on.

A boyhood thought jumped into his mind: *"I'm a secret agent!"* He'd read James Fenimore Cooper's book, 'The Spy' and in earlier years had acted out some of the hero's adventures. Now, he was part of a *real* adventure.

With a shiver of excitement Henry realised he was in an ideal position to see and hear everything that was going on.

Through the door to the courtyard, he could hear the mumble of reporters gathered around the scaffold. And through the door to the corridor, he could make out another voice: that of Richard Burgess. Spy fantasies left Henry's head as pulled the door open a crack, and strained to listen.

Burgess's cell was only a few paces further up the corridor, and even though Burgess was speaking quietly, Henry could follow most of his words.

"Christian friend," Burgess said, "Most willingly I write to you, thanking you for your kind and Christian-like letter."

Who's he writing to?

Henry put his ear against the crack in the door – then leapt back as a dark shape blocked the light. It was the hangman, hovering outside Burgess's cell door.

Horrible man!

There was a mumble of conversation in the corridor, and another figure appeared. Henry recognised Warder Jolly. He was holding something behind his back. It was a small posy of flowers, and Jolly held it only a few inches from Henry's nose. Henry peered through the crack.

He saw a sprig of deep crimson mānuka flowers, small but intense, fastened to an intricate fern frond. And stems of fragrant lavender, alongside three frilly pink Carnea roses.

He also recognized a tiny edelweiss, unusual for this time of year. Someone had spent a good deal of time finding these flowers and arranging them into a small bouquet. *I wonder who?*

A-choo!! The sneeze came so suddenly that Henry had no time to stifle it. *Oh, no! Did anyone hear me?* He scuttled back into the corner of the storeroom, and pressed his finger beneath his nose to stop the next sneeze. It ended in a snuffle.

Did they hear me? The spy in the cupboard?

In the corridor, someone muttered. Henry couldn't hear the words. Then Burgess's voice broke through.

"Sweet soul, rest assured," he read aloud, "though my pulse will have ceased to beat in the hand that answers yours, I trust that it will be beating in Heaven."

"Most eloquent and spiritual," said the Reverend Hadfield.

Then Warder Jolly's gruff voice: "Here, Burgess, take these."

"Flowers!" cried Burgess.

"Yeah, some fool loves ya."

"Let me finish my last letter," said Burgess. He spoke quietly: "May God, in His wonderful kindness, ever bless you. Yours in Christ. Richard Burgess."

"Come on, Burgess," said the warder.

Burgess ignored him. "Reverend," he said, "would you be kind enough to make sure this letter reaches its home?"

"Certainly," said the minister.

"Now I am ready to face my maker," Burgess announced. Henry heard the rattle of chains and crept to the gap in the door.

He saw a swirl of black as the masked hangman entered Burgess's cell.

"Here, lemme unlock these," the man grunted. More sounds of chains clanging.

Shortly Warder Jolly emerged into the corridor, pushing Burgess ahead of him.

Henry was certain they would see him as he pressed his face close to the crack. But he couldn't help himself. He had to see this criminal – this man who called himself his father – being marched to his death.

As Burgess shuffled past, Henry saw his arms had been tied behind his back – tight enough to prevent any violent movement, but loose enough for him to reach out.

In one hand, Burgess held the posy of flowers.

Henry grimaced at the cold clanging of the prison bell.

The end of the world was near for Burgess and his mates.

Burgess picked up his posy of flowers. He would
hold them for the rest of his life.

Warder Jolly and the executioner escorted Burgess down the corridor. Henry swivelled his neck as far as he could, and in the sunlight, framed by the open door, he could see three nooses swaying above the scaffold.

This is horrible! I can't bear it. Henry screwed his eyes shut. He tasted a small dribble of vomit in his mouth.

FORTY
PRELUDE TO HEAVEN

IN THE DARKNESS OF THE STOREROOM, HENRY LEANT AGAINST the wall and tried to settle his breathing. By some twist of fate, he had found himself a secret witness to a gruesome event. Three men were about to be hung by their necks until their breathing stopped. And one of those men was possibly his father.

Henry could have retreated down the corridor to the back of the prison. He could have sat in a corner and waited until it was all over. Instead, he went to the door that led to the courtyard, and turned the handle.

Bit by bit, his heart pounding, he unlocked the door and pulled it open. Ever so slightly. Just enough to get a clear view. He peered out.

Nelson Prison seemed almost cheerful in the early morning sun, and Richard Burgess was likewise cheerful as he emerged from the cells, holding his flowers. Henry saw Kelly there too, muttering feverishly. And Levy, impassive and expressionless. These men who had once held Henry captive, laughed at his discomfort, and gone on to murder five men in the hills, were now themselves miserable captives.

Henry twisted to see Burgess. There he was, grinning at the small crowd of officials and reporters who hovered around the scaffold. *How can he look so happy!?* Burgess shook hands with Kelly and Levy, and proclaimed, "Well, companions in misfortune, this is the last day of our lives."

Burgess's face was flushed, and his eyes, which could look so frightening, now seemed to flash with excitement.

Burgess shook hands with everyone, including Major Shallcrass, who had been promoted to inspector because of his handling of the now-famous Maungatapu Murders case.

Henry looked around. He could see reporters following close to Burgess, scribbling down his every word.

Aware of this attention, Burgess said to Sergeant Nash, "I hope you will continue in the same upright course that you have hitherto pursued, and in showing humanity to all you have occasion to arrest."

And as Warder Jolly took his arm to steer him towards the gallows, Burgess thanked him for his "gentle" approach. "This is better than treating prisoners harshly, which embitters and maddens them, and in their souls they curse their keeper."

To everyone in the courtyard, Burgess announced loudly:

"Here is a great sinner of thirty-eight years' standing going to his account, and so much am I assured of the loving-kindness of the Saviour, who has said 'though your sins be as scarlet, I can make them as white as snow', that although going to that fatal scaffold, I feel as happy as if I were going to a wedding this bright and beautiful morning."

Henry blinked. *What a speech! What a crazy thing to say!*

"This is the morning of my death," Burgess continued, "but it is also the morning of my birth into another and a brighter world, where sorrow shall pass away, and all tears be wiped from my eyes.

"I am ready to obey the commands of the law. I pray that God will have mercy on my soul."

Henry could see onlookers shaking their heads in amazement. *No wonder!*

Henry lowered himself to his knees. He was certain no one would notice him peering through the crack in the door, especially when he was down at the level of their legs.

Maybe I can just... He pushed the door slightly wider, and could see everything more clearly.

Here comes Johnny Slick! The dime novelist came so close to the door that Henry could have reached out and touched the caked mud on the man's trousers.

"Well, well, well," said Slick, "if it isn't James Phillimore Abercrombie!"

"Johnny Slick!" A smaller man in a smart suit came into view. "Why am I not surprised to find you here?"

"My readers demand it," said Slick. "They will want every detail, bless their souls. And this man – Burgess – what an orator!"

"Aye, he is that," said Abercrombie. "And he's about to give the last performance of his bloody career."

"Nooooo!" A chilling cry took them all by surprise. It was Kelly. Shaking and moaning, he took out several sheets of paper filled with his writing, and began to read. His speech was slurred.

"He's drunk!" said Abercrombie.

"No," said a minister nearby, who had spent time with Kelly. "He is tired. And demented."

Kelly launched into his prepared speech. "You are spectators of one of the most awful, terrible, dreadful, fearful, shameful, painful, mournful, sorrowful, hateful…"

Despite the grim setting, Henry could not help smiling at Kelly's string of adjectives.

"… wrongful and unjustifiable, ignominious, inglorious deaths and murders that ever took place in the wide world since the creation of Adam."

Burgess shook his head. "Don't lose your self-respect, man."

Kelly would not be stopped. "May God be merciful to me, a sinner."

After his speech, Kelly handed his notes to the sheriff and collapsed onto a bench. "God bless us all. I have cried all night to myself, and I can't cry now."

Levy also delivered a long speech, and ended: "I declare to the Almighty in Heaven, and to this assembly, that I am innocent. Amen!"

Henry nodded. He recalled that although Levy had been at the scene of the murders, he seemed the least violent of all the gang. But Slick and Abercrombie exchanged cynical looks.

Henry was trembling at the drama and excitement of the occasion. He had read many adventure stories, but none as gripping as this. The sight of the ropes swinging on the scaffold reminded him that this was real. Three real men faced a real death. He gulped.

Warder Jolly moved to escort Burgess to the scaffold, but the condemned man bounded up the steps by himself. It was as though he was stepping onto the stage of a theatre, with a captive audience. Perhaps that was how he saw it.

Kelly did not want to follow. "I'm innocent!" he cried out in a pitiful voice.

Burgess barked: "Shut up, Kelly, and die like a man!"

Henry watched, wide-eyed, as Kelly started up the long staircase to the gallows. "I am innocent! Don't be in a hurry!" His legs buckled under him, and Warder Jolly and a guard had to carry him up the steps.

Burgess walked to the middle noose and took hold of it. *Here is my father!* Henry checked himself. *I still don't know. I will never know.* Burgess acknowledged his "audience" – Slick, Abercrombie, and the other reporters, gathered near the scaffold with their notebooks poised. Then Burgess looked towards Henry's door. *Is he looking at me? He can't be.* Henry drew back, but quickly returned to the door.

Burgess kissed the noose and cried out theatrically, "I greet you as a prelude to Heaven!"

A prelude to Heaven? Henry frowned. He saw reporters making notes. Abercrombie leant over to Slick and whispered: "What a quote!"

Then a scream—

Kelly was yelling, "Please Lord, no!"

Henry stood up for a better view, and looked out through the crack. The three condemned men now had their arms bound to their sides and their feet tied together at the ankles. They knelt with their backs to the front of the platform. The executioner placed a rope around their necks.

"I'm not hanged," Kelly cried out, "I'm murdered!"

Warder Jolly put a white cap on him.

Burgess remained calm. He knelt, the noose around his neck.

Henry saw that tough old Warder Jolly was close to tears, but Burgess reassured him. "I die, and I deserve my fate." He bent to allow the warder to pull the white cap over his head.

Reporters and the small group of official witnesses waited, ashen-faced.

Henry thought he might be sick.

The Reverend Hadfield stood close by, reading a prayer to Burgess, who quietly repeated every word.

And then…

The hangman's hand reached for the lever.

Pulled it.

All the speechifying and wailing came to a sudden end.

THUNK! Three living bodies dropped from the platform.

Burgess still held the flowers.

SNAP! Three ropes twanged tight. Three bodies jerked to a stop.

Henry stopped breathing. His finger nails bit into his face.

Everyone in the crowd flinched.

Warder Jolly turned away and wiped his eyes.

In his dark hideaway, Henry gagged. He stumbled to a corner of the room and fell on his knees. Vomit welled up in his throat, then spewed onto the floor.

"Oh, no!" Abercrombie's cry made Henry turn. *What now?* He crawled to the door, aware he had vomit on his trousers.

He could see the bodies of his "father" and two accomplices swinging from the beam, their bodies twisting lazily in the morning sun. The small crowd of grim-faced witnesses watched in silence.

Slick and Abercrombie were staring at Kelly. He was still alive. His legs kicked as he fought for breath.

"How ghastly," said Abercrombie.

Onlookers gasped as the hangman raced down the scaffold steps and swung on Kelly's legs to hasten his death.

A bespectacled clerk in the crowd fainted.

One of the official observers rushed to a corner to vomit.

Johnny Slick scribbled in his notebook. "We are told," he read aloud to Abercrombie, "that in the moments before you die, your life flashes before your eyes. If this is true, what images flashed through the mind of Richard Burgess?"

"He sees the faces of the men he has killed," said Abercrombie. "Surely."

Henry wondered too. There had been moments when Burgess seemed evil, but other moments when he… well, *he looked at me like he was my father.*

"Is it possible," Abercrombie mused, "that Burgess did indeed 'find the Lord'?"

"And asked God to forgive a lifetime of unspeakable violence? Most unlikely."

"Why would he bother then, with all that religious talk?"

"Perhaps because it's theatrical."

"Probably. This was his last Royal performance."

"I wish I'd been given the opportunity to talk to the man," said Slick. "He is – he was – a most extraordinary creature."

Henry took a deep breath. *Don't talk about him like that! He's still alive!* He looked over at Burgess's body, and saw Burgess's fingers tremble as his muscles fought for oxygen.

He watched as Burgess's hand relaxed in death. His fingers released the flowers, and they floated down, down, down… until they hit the ground and scattered.

It seemed like Burgess had held the flowers forever, reluctant to bid them farewell.

Abercrombie held up his fob watch. "Twenty-five seconds," he breathed.

"Has his heart stopped pumping?" Slick whispered to Abercrombie.

"They say the brain will live on for several minutes."

The sky darkened over Nelson Prison.

The lifeless bodies of Richard Burgess, Thomas Kelly, and Philip Levy swayed from their ropes. Terrifying highwaymen no more.

They're just like three sacks of potatoes.

Henry slumped against the wall and closed his eyes. *I'll never be able to get this out of my head.*

"Listen to this," said Abercrombie: "This morning the awful sentence of the law was carried into execution on these wretched malefactors."

"Is that what you've written? A bit pompous," said Slick. "Nevertheless, I might borrow it."

"I'm sure you will," said Abercrombie.

People around them began to chatter, and Henry peered

out again. The courtyard sprang back into life. As if released from a spell, observers began to share their thoughts. Feelings of disgust, awe, or relief.

My father is dead, thought Henry. A murderer, a troubled soul, a man who brought misery to many. *But still – maybe – my father.*

He looked up and saw Johnny Slick making furious notes. His hand was shaky. *Too many whiskeys for breakfast.*

"We've seen our fair share of hangings, you and I," he said to Abercrombie.

"And been sickened by each and every one," said his friend.

"But our readers will find our descriptions fascinating, even romantic."

"If only they knew."

Abercrombie slipped his notebook into his pocket. "You back to the States now?"

"No, no, I still have some assignments to complete."

"Oh? I thought your lecture tour was over."

"It is," said Slick, "but..." He pulled out a well-worn *carte de visite.*

Henry bit his lip. That was *his* precious souvenir that Slick was waving around.

"Von Tempsky?" Abercrombie snorted. "What do you want with that scoundrel?"

"The man's a folk hero," said Slick, "whether you like him or not."

"He's brave, I'll give him that," said Abercrombie. "But methinks he doth blow his own trumpet too loud."

"Perhaps," laughed Slick. "But he provides excellent copy, and my readers love a swashbuckler."

"Swashbuckler? Is that even a word?"

Slick chuckled and put away the postcard.

"I travel to Auckland next week to pay him a visit."

"He'll be glad to have a ready listener," said Abercrombie. "Farewell, my friend."

He joined the crowds out on the street, and Slick turned to watch prison staff get the bodies of the hanged men down from the gallows. Warder Jolly began to herd the observers out of the courtyard. He took one last look at Burgess's limp body and left.

In his dark cell, Henry began shaking. He could not stop himself. His hands trembled. His leg quivered. He was sweating. *I've got to get out of here!*

He climbed to his feet, supporting himself against the wall.

Slick had no doubt this was Doctor Z. Smith.

"Well I never!" exclaimed Slick. Henry looked out and followed Slick's gaze.

On the nearby hill, the figure of a lone horseman was

silhouetted against the sky. The man was sitting straight-backed on his horse.

"Doctor Z. Smith, if I'm not mistaken."

He was not mistaken. Henry knew for sure it was the doctor. *He's back from Australia! I wonder if Miriama is with him?*

The figure watched as the black flag fluttered at the top of the prison flagpole. Then he flicked the reins and galloped away.

"Excellent!" Slick exclaimed. "What a gothic image!" He licked his pencil and quickly sketched.

"It'll add a poetic touch to my next dime novel. Don't you agree, Henry?"

Henry backed away. Slick stuck his boot in the doorway and pushed it open.

"This was a goddam awful spectacle for a young man to witness," he said in a low voice. "I trust ya have a strong stomach."

Henry grabbed his walking stick, retreated into the storeroom, then wrenched open the door to the corridor, and raced towards the back entrance.

Duke was snoozing in the sun, and snorted as Henry appeared and untied the reins. Henry struggled onto the horse's back, wincing as he pulled his injured leg across the saddle.

"Git!" They trotted away from the prison. *Goodbye, Burgess, whoever you are.*

He saw Chadwick and Luxton coming towards him, their buggy full of boxes. It was too late to avoid them.

More vultures. What do they want?

Chadwick called out as they passed. "See you at the auction, boy."

Henry ignored him. *My parents taught me to offer kindness to everyone. Why is everyone I meet so unkind?*

Henry rode on, Chadwick's wheezing cackle in his ears, and spurred Duke into a gallop. On the hilltop overlooking the prison, he pulled up. There was no sign of Doctor Smith.

It was still early morning, but above the gothic jail, dark clouds had rolled across the sky. It could have been evening.

FORTY-ONE
A HIDDEN MESSAGE

DUKE AND HENRY GALLOPED ACROSS THE OPEN SPACE, PAST the chapel, and came to a stop at the cemetery.

Henry's mind was swirling with sounds and images of the hanging. He had just seen Richard Burgess die a grisly death, and now he knew where he wanted to go. Where he needed to go. He stopped by the grave of William Henry Appleton, the man who had raised him and passed on his values.

William Appleton may not have been his birth father, but he was the man who had given Henry the love and security he needed.

I want to be like you, Father, not like Burgess. He slumped in the saddle. *Why did Burgess have to come into my life?*

He rested his head on Duke's neck and thought about his last visit with Burgess in prison. The man had pleaded with him to call him 'father', but he couldn't. And he had made him a gift.

The gift! Henry remembered the parchment, still folded

in his pocket. He wiped his eyes, unfurled it, and squinted to read the intricate handwriting:

Ecclesiastes chapter 9, verse 10: "Whatsoever thy hand findeth to do –"

As he read it, he could hear the voice of Burgess:

"… do it wiv thy might, for there is no work, nor device, nor knowledge, nor wisdom in the grave wither thou goest."

Henry puzzled the relevance. *Why did Burgess write this?* He heard Burgess's voice as he resumed reading.

"He that loveth silver shall not be satisfied wiv silver. Instead shall thou find great treasure beneath the tree where first thy life was spared."

Henry stiffened. *These words are not from the Bible.* He looked again. *Beneath the tree?* The drawing alongside the text showed a figure digging beneath a tree. Nearby, another figure was sprawled on the ground.

That's me! A horse. *That's Duke!* And an egg. *That's where Burgess jumped out at me.*

The truth dawned on him like a slap in the face, and he laughed out loud. "Of course!" He reached down and grabbed the handle of a shovel stuck in the earth near his father's grave. A phrase caught his eye:

Learn to do good; seek justice.

He galloped off and plunged into the dark forest, slowing only to navigate the twisted undergrowth. Here was the track where the ghosts of Burgess and Sullivan had pursued him.

Was it only a few months ago?

Finally, he came to the spot where Burgess had ambushed him. He slithered from the saddle and saw a dead shrub at the base of the tree. He tossed it aside. The soil was freshly turned. *This must be it.* He stabbed at it with the shovel. He half-knelt, awkward with his stiff leg. Scraped soil away. It was hard work.

"Treasure of great worth"? What could it be?

He glanced above and about him: it seemed the giant trees were staring down at him. *What are you looking at?* He continued to scoop out the earth and throw it aside. Feverish now. His leg was aching, but he could not stop.

"Thou shall find great treasure beneath the tree where first thy life was spared." Henry could hardly breathe with excitement.

Finally, success: he dragged out a box.

"Yes!" *This is it!* He could hardly breathe with excitement as he wrenched the box open. Inside was a small sack tied with a cord. With shaking hands, he pulled it open.

There, lying before him, was a small pile of gold nuggets.

Treasure!

Some nuggets were no bigger than a pea, but many were the size of a walnut.

They resembled bits of crumpled volcanic rock, except for their telltale dull yellow colouring. Soon they would be cleaned and polished and fashioned into precious bars or jewellery.

Henry scooped up a handful. *I'm rich!*

He shouted in the air, "Thank you, Burgess! Thank you, God!"

I can buy the farm!

Henry paused to glower at the trees that crowded above him. Then he allowed the nuggets to tumble from his fingers, glinting in the sun, and back into the sack. He tied the cord at the neck of the sack and threw it over Duke's saddle.

FORTY-TWO
TEMPTATION

HENRY'S HEART WAS POUNDING AS HE RODE TOWARDS Bluebell Cottage with the bag of gold slung across the saddle.

We're rich! We can buy the farm!

There was a horse tied up outside. *Who is here?*

He covered the sack of gold with a blanket and held it by his side as he entered the cottage. There in the kitchen, chatting with Henry's mother, was Doctor Zephaniah Smith.

Henry had not spoken to Smith since the doctor had brought his fingerprinting gear into prison and discovered that Burgess was not the man who killed his wife.

He had seen Smith on the hill overlooking the prison. And now, here he was.

Hide the gold!

"Doctor Smith!" Henry strode forward to greet him, flicking the blanket-covered sack into the corner.

Smith smiled and grasped Henry's hand. "Henry!"

"It is wonderful to see you, sir."

"How is your sketching, Henry?"

Smith had not let go of Henry's hand.

"Ah – I haven't been doing that so much lately. I –"

"Perhaps you have your mind set on a new career?"

"A new career?"

Henry peered out into the garden.

Is Miriama here? He searched his mother's face.

"Yes, a career as a physician, Henry. I believe it is your calling."

"A physician? Ah –"

"A painter can reflect the world, Henry, but a physician can help to change it."

"Mmm."

Doctor Smith chuckled. "You have your mind on something else, I can see." He released his grip and pointed out into the garden. "Yes, I have brought Miriama home."

Henry turned and saw her, out in the back yard.

"Miriama!"

He did not immediately run out to see her: Miriama was standing at the fence line, talking to two elderly Māori women on Chadwick's land.

"Who are they?" he asked his mother.

"Miriama's aunties. They've come to see that she is well."

Henry watched impatiently as Miriama pressed noses with the two women, who then turned and walked off towards a larger group of Māori men and women further up the slope. He ran into the garden.

"Miriama!"

She turned: a young woman, no longer dressed as a man.

You are beautiful.

"Henry!" She looked at his stiff leg and the walking stick. "Are you in pain?" she asked.

"I'm getting used to it." He pulled her towards him and embraced her.

She melted into him.

"Are you here to stay?"

Miriama nodded, smiling.

"We can set up home, Miriama," he blurted out. But she held up her palm in a "stop" sign.

"After we see the Queen."

"The Queen?"

"Yes," said Miriama. "She needs to know what is happening."

"What is happening?"

"The kiore – our native rat. It's being pushed out by the white man's rat."

"What's the rat got to do with anything?" *Can't we talk about you and me?*

"The same thing is happening to my people," said Miriama.

"What – you're getting pushed out by rats?"

"No, Henry. But so many white people are coming to Aotearoa. And Māori are losing their land, their culture. Everything."

"It doesn't need to be that way," Henry countered. "Surely."

Miriama nodded. "I choose to believe there is hope."

Why are we talking about these things? He put on a bright face and stood back to admire Miriama.

She gave a small smile. "No more hiding. No more…

mask." Her slender fingers demonstrated a veil being drawn aside.

"I'm glad," said Henry. "Very glad."

He turned at the sound of Smith's horse galloping away. *Good – no questions about the gold.*

He looked into Miriama's eyes. "Miriama – something wonderful! I haven't told mother yet, but –" He checked his mother was busy in the kitchen. "I've got enough gold to pay for the farm! We won't have to sell it."

"Gold?" Miriama's smile froze.

"Yes. It was a gift. From a friend."

"A friend?" Miriama removed her hands from his.

Should I tell her?

"Burgess," he said.

"Burgess!" Miriama backed away.

"Yes, Burgess," said Henry. "He wants me to have it."

Why isn't she excited? "We can buy the farm!"

Miriama pursed her lips.

"The gold – this is a good thing he's done," said Henry. "It's his dying wish – for me – for us! So we can save the farm."

Miriama narrowed her eyes. "And how did Burgess get the gold?"

"Can't you be excited for us?" Henry took a quick look at his mother, busy in the kitchen. "This'll change our lives."

Miriama dropped her eyes to study the ground.

"The men who found the gold are dead," argued Henry. "They don't need it. And we do."

He touched Miriama's hand. She pulled away.

His mother called from the cottage. "Miriama?"

"It'll break her heart if she loses the farm," Henry hissed.

Miriama gave him a long look. "Better to lose the farm than lose your soul," she said.

Lose my soul? "Is that another one of your 'proverbs'?" Henry stalked off to the far end of the garden and poked the dirt with his walking stick.

Miriama went back inside the cottage. Henry looked around, muttering, at the hens pecking in the dirt. Alberta needed hay. The vegetables were struggling. The fence sagged. *We are so poor. The gold will change everything.*

In the cottage, the two women looked out at Henry as he paced around. His mother put an arm around Miriama. Henry glared at them. He hobbled to the fence and contemplated the broken section. *Yes, yes – I'll fix it tomorrow.*

He flicked weeds with his walking stick and saw, clinging to a rock, a tiny South Island edelweiss. It was not yet summer, but there it was – a delicate flower shining cheerily among the weeds. He glowered at it.

Someone had placed an edelweiss in the posy Burgess held in the moments before he died. *Is this a sign? What does it mean?*

Thoughts of Burgess and his gang hammered at his brain. The threats. The violence. The screams of the dying men. Burgess's own confessions. The gang huddled around their campfire, examining the gold for which they had slaughtered four men.

Henry licked his dry lips.

He looked up to see Miriama and his mother watching him from the kitchen window.

Yes, I know. There's blood on that gold.

He straightened up, drew his breath, and returned to the cottage.

He walked into the kitchen. "You're right," he said. "The gold should be returned to the murdered men's families."

He took Miriama's hand. "We may lose the farm, but it won't be the end of the world."

Miriama squeezed his hand and smiled.

"We will manage," said his mother calmly. "And look." She lifted Smith's leather bag onto the table. "Doctor Smith said it was yours."

Henry stared at the doctor's bag with its distinctive bullet hole, and the embossed 'Z. Smith'. He grinned. *That bag and I have had some terrifying adventures!*

Inside the bag was a sturdy, leather-bound book. Henry lifted it out and examined the title: *A Manual of General Anatomy of the Human Body*.

"Doctor Smith seems convinced that you'll make a fine doctor," said his mother.

"You don't sound so sure, mother."

"No no, I am. Far better to be a physician than a writer of dime novels."

Henry bit his lip. He took the stethoscope out of the bag, put the ear tips to his head, and spoke into the diaphragm. "Doctor Appleton will now see his patients," he said in his deepest voice. *Perhaps one day?*

The women giggled.

"Doctor Smith has promised to help us," said his mother.

"What do you mean –'us'?"

"He said he will help us buy the farm."

"Buy the farm?" Henry gasped.

"Yes," said his mother. "Buy the farm and never see that nasty man Chadwick again." She pulled Miriama and Henry towards her. "We have much to be grateful for." She closed her eyes in prayer. "Dear Lord, we thank you for our good fortune."

They all said "Amen!" with conviction.

"And," Henry's mother continued, "we pray for the souls of the men who were hanged today."

"Also," said Miriama in a quiet voice, "we pray that Burgess might receive forgiveness."

Henry saw, held between Miriama's fingers, a tiny flower – a South Island edelweiss. *Strange!* But he had no time to dwell on it.

FORTY-THREE
WHAT KIND OF MEN?

In their cottage, Henry, his mother, and Miriama bowed their heads in prayer for the condemned men.

Henry relived it in his mind: the jail, the swinging corpses, the black flag. Once he had imagined it would be romantic to be a dime novelist like Johnny Slick. *Not anymore.* He would never want to write about this.

He knew he would continue to have nightmares about the gang. *Especially Sullivan.* Nightmares about the way Burgess had murdered so many men, but also the manner in which Burgess met his own death.

Worse still, Henry had been told what would now happen to the bodies of the three hanged men. They would be handed over to the local phrenologists – men like Chadwick and Luxton, who were convinced the shape of a man's skull could reveal the secrets of his character. Although most scientists scoffed at their beliefs, the phrenologists had enough followers to fill the meeting halls when they lectured.

And now they had access to the skulls of three infamous highwaymen to showcase their beliefs.

Burgess, Levy and Kelly – reduced to scientific oddities. The thought dismayed Henry.

He tried not to imagine the three macabre plaster cast heads sitting in a row. Eyes shut. Emotionless. Frozen forever at the moment of death.

He knew that forever more, these death masks would be on show at the town museum. They would thrill and horrify thousands of curious visitors, who would ponder, "What kind of men were these? What made them do what they did?"

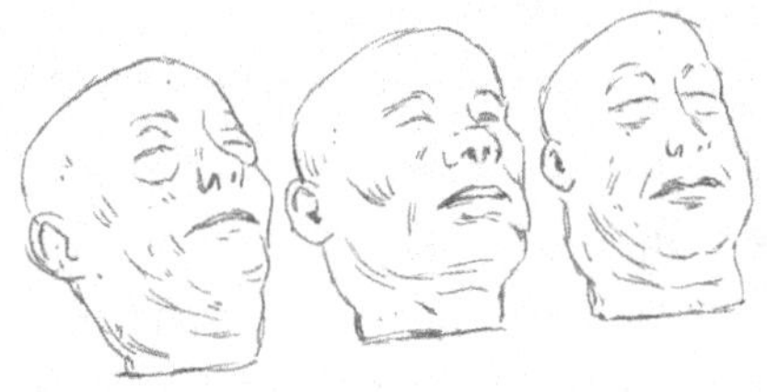

FORTY-FOUR
NOT FORGOTTEN

It was October 1866. It had been less than six months since the Burgess gang had arrived in Nelson. They had murdered five men in the hills, they had been tried by jury, and three of them had been hanged.

So it was that late in the evening, in a bleak corner of the Nelson Prison courtyard, two guards shovelled the last few piles of dirt onto three graves.

The guards' shadows performed a ghoulish dance on the rough bricks of the courtyard walls.

Nature herself had designed a gothic setting for this occasion. The moon was just a sliver, and among the leafy evergreens visible just beyond the prison walls, one diseased oak tree stood out.

It was springtime, but instead of displaying fresh leaves, the ravaged branches of this old oak were bare. They appeared to be reaching out to claw their way over the walls and into the prison.

Henry Appleton, huddled in a jacket, leant on his

walking stick at the edge of the yard and watched the guards.

How can anyone know who the villains are? A "good" man can be corrupted. An evil man can have an insight from God.

One grave had a wooden cross, on which there was a crudely written inscription. It said simply: *R. Burgess. Murderer.*

The guards finished their work. One of them spat on Burgess's grave. Then they took their shovels and shuffled away.

Our account draws to a close late in the evening, in a bleak corner of the Nelson Prison courtyard.

Henry approached. *Burgess followed a path of crime. I choose a different life.* He repeated it aloud, for the benefit of the twisted oak tree and the cold prison walls. "I choose a different path!"

He pulled a wildflower from his pocket and crouched at

Burgess's grave. "Father," he said quietly. "If you are. If you were…"

Behind him, someone coughed. He swung around.

In the shadows at the end of the courtyard was Johnny Slick, his long coat wrapped around him and his hat pulled low. "*Was* he your father?" he asked.

"What are you doing here?" Henry demanded.

"This is the end of a chapter," said the American.

"This is not a 'story'," said Henry. "It's a real life. And this is a private moment."

The men stood silent for a long moment, staring at each other, before Henry spoke again. "Possibly he was my father, yes. But I'll never know. Nor do I care. I've chosen a different path. "

"You've written your own story," said Slick.

Henry nodded. "I have."

Slick gave a slight bow. "Goodbye, Henry Appleton."

He withdrew into the shadows. Henry heard the gate click behind him. He turned back to Burgess's grave.

He placed the wildflower against the cross and pulled his jacket around him.

Time would soon wipe away the physical remains of the murderer who had claimed to be Henry's father. Henry's wildflower would wither. Autumn leaves would fall, and the wind would whip them away. Sleet and snow would drift down and cover the cross. The writing would fade. The cross would eventually rot and drop into the mud.

In years to come, there would be no official record of where Burgess's body had been laid to rest.

But his name would live on – longer than the names of

the men he killed, or the judge who sentenced him, or the hangman who dispatched him.

Books would be written about him, and visitors to the Provincial Museum would gather around his death mask as their teachers recounted Burgess's bloody story.

The judge had predicted that Burgess would never be admired as a "hero of crime". But Burgess's eloquent and chilling confession would continue to fascinate people, and would ensure that he was not forgotten.

Not admired, certainly, but not forgotten.

EPILOGUE

MOSTLY TRUE

"DOCTOR APPLETON, YOU THERE?"

It is now 1875, nine years since the Maungatapu Murders.

A young postal clerk, Jimmy O'Shaunessey, stands at the door of a modest wooden office building, clutching a leather satchel to his chest.

He raps on the door again. A freshly painted shingle hangs from hooks above the door, swaying in the breeze: *Henry Appleton. Physician.*

Jimmy has heard stories of kidnapping and murder up in the hills, and he knows Henry Appleton was involved. While he waits for the doctor, he looks around.

Across the road in a shop window he spots a gruesome display: the plaster casts of three human heads, lined up like sideshow clowns at a fair. But there is no laughter here: these are death masks.

"Jeepers!" He ducks in front of a slow-moving horse and cart and crosses the street for a closer look.

The sign reads: *Death masks of the Maungatapu Murderers. Lecture tonight! Admission One Shilling.*

The plaster cast heads are shaven and macabre, their eyes sightless. As a passing cart blocks out the sunlight, the eyes of the death masks momentarily flicker into life. The clerk jumps backwards.

"Jimmy!"

He doesn't look around. He knows the voice – it is the doctor – but he can't let those eerie heads out of his sight. Their eyes keep glaring at him as he backs away.

"Oi!" a farmer yells at him as he nearly falls under the hooves of a pair of Clydesdale horses hauling a wagon.

"That was close, Jimmy."

The boy grins. Everyone likes Doc Henry. "He's seen things," his mother once told him. Whatever that meant. Seen what things?

"It's true, isn't it, Doc – you met them?"

Henry Appleton looks over at the masks, lifeless but potent. "Met them? I certainly did." He rubs the scar on his jaw. "Now – Jimmy?"

"Oh, yes. Sorry, Doc." From his satchel, Jimmy hauls out the envelope. "It's from the United States of America."

"So it is, Jimmy."

"I've been wondering what's inside."

Henry smiles. "Well, let's find out, shall we?"

He takes the envelope. They both peer at the sender's name, and the young clerk asks the question that has been on his lips all morning. "Who's Johnny Slick?"

"An old friend," says Henry.

He brings out his pocketknife, slits open the envelope, and pauses. *Could it be?*

It is. After all these years, Johnny Slick's dime novel.

Jimmy has seen these little paperbacks before, at Mr Tingle's bookshop on Bridge Street: adventure stories from America, mostly about cowboys and Indians.

He looks closer at the magazine. On the cover there is a brightly painted illustration of a young man leaping at an older man who wields a pistol.

Henry chuckles at the glamorised depiction of his fight with Kelly in the Pritchard cottage.

There is a note attached to the book, and he reads it aloud.

To my young hero. Finally, I get to tell a story that's mostly true.

Jimmy is impressed. "Doc – that's you!"

He points at the cover and reads aloud, slowly: "Henry Appleton – Boy Hero!"

"Don't believe everything you read in these dime novels, Jimmy."

The boy doesn't hear him. He reads on: *A true adventure story from Johnny Slick.*

"Wait till I tell the lads!" He skips off down the street, swinging the empty mail satchel around his head.

Henry gives his departing fan a half smile. *I was a lad then. But that was a lifetime ago.*

It was, in fact, only nine years ago, and he remembers it all with a chilling clarity. He remembers the crisp winter skies. The dense forests echoing with the voices of myriad birds.

The physician, Zephaniah Smith.

And despite his best efforts to wipe them from his

memory, he remembers Burgess and Sullivan. They live in his nightmares.

He drops the dime novel into Smith's old leather bag and coils his stethoscope on top. With his finger, he traces the outline of the bullet hole.

So close!

He shuts the office door and looks up at the sign:

Henry Appleton. Physician.

He taps the sign. "Zephaniah Smith, thank you!"

The doctor never returned, but he gave the Appletons the money to buy their cottage. And true to his word, he also paid for Henry to go to college. Henry is now a physician, just like the man who changed his life forever.

Henry – Doctor Henry – crosses the street.

In the shop window he sees the death masks of Burgess, Kelly, and Levy, and pauses to study them. The men who terrorised him are now lifeless sculptures.

"Evening, Doc," says a chirpy voice behind him.

Jimmy the postal clerk and the shopkeeper O'Shaunessey join him at the window.

O'Shaunessey points at the sign: *Lecture tonight!* "Will we be seein' you there tonight, Doc?"

Doc Henry imitates his friend's Irish brogue. "Not on your life, O'Shaunessey. Not on your life." He smiles and heads off.

"The Doc was there, Father," says Jimmy. He points at the death masks. "He met them."

"Did he indeed, son."

Henry accepts that the evil exploits of the Burgess gang will continue to be the subject of newspaper articles and books.

But he and the good folk of Nelson prefer to focus on the gang's victims: the five innocent men they slaughtered in the hills above Nelson.

The townspeople have paid for a large granite obelisk to be built in the local graveyard. Its inscription reads: *Erected by the citizens of Nelson, in memory of the victims of the Maungatapu Murderers. 1866.*

This evening, on his way home on Duke, Henry takes a long detour to the Wakapuaka Cemetery, and there, high on the hill, he pauses in front of the monument.

His eyes rest on one phrase: *Vengeance is mine – I will repay, saith the Lord.* Is that true, he wonders?

He looks around at the granite headstones scattered across the gentle slopes of the cemetery. This is the last resting place of respectable Nelson settlers who lived into old age, but also of children who did not live beyond the cradle.

They are at peace now, the newer headstones sparkling

in the crisp evening light, the older headstones beginning to crumble, with weeds forcing up between the cracks.

We all end up here, muses Henry. *How many of us will be remembered?*

Burgess and his gang are still talked about, their names more familiar than those of their hapless victims. *What does that say about us?*

"Doctor Appleton!"

A short distance away, a smartly dressed gentleman waves in Henry's direction.

"Mister Canning! What brings –"

"Planting trees, naturally." Charles Canning chuckles, and gestures towards three workers who are leaning on shovels nearby. "Planting trees. It's my besetting sin – but hopefully a pardonable one."

Henry slides off Duke, and the two men shake hands.

"You'll long be remembered for the many trees you've gifted to the town, sir."

"Do you think so?" asks the older man. "There's an adage: 'The evil which man does lives after him, but the good is oft interred with his bones.'"

"A gloomy thought," says Henry. He indicates the memorial obelisk. "I had just been musing on the same theme myself. The names of Burgess and Sullivan are well known. But not their victims'."

"Burgess – what a fascinating man," says Canning. "Evil, of course, but with his own twisted sense of right and wrong."

Henry nods. *Burgess. Probably my father. But Charles Canning doesn't need to know.*

He recalls Charles Canning and the other jurors listening wide-eyed as Burgess read his "Confessions".

The two men stand in silence. Then Henry asks:

"How is your boy William, sir?"

"Still poorly, I'm afraid. Perhaps you would be kind enough to pay us a visit this week."

"I shall, sir."

"And stay for dinner," says Canning. "Well – back to my little oak trees."

Henry bids him farewell, and watches as the farmer and his workers resume their digging. More oak trees; more reminders of the country they still call home.

He rides back towards town, before veering into the familiar fields. Past the chapel, through the forest that still features in his nightmares, past Murderers' Rock, and finally home.

He hears a small boy's voice cry out "Pow, Pow!" and recalls the days when he himself was desperate to own a gun. *Not anymore.*

He rides up to the farm. *Bluebell Cottage.* The familiar nameplate, somewhat faded, still hangs on the porch.

A boy of six is leaning out the window with a toy wooden gun. "Pow, pow!"

Miriama is working with Henry's mother in the garden. There are beans, cabbages, kūmara, potatoes, and pumpkins… gooseberries, rhubarb and sweet corn… a small orchard of apple and plum trees… and rows of lavender, mint, rosemary, and sage.

The oak tree they planted soon after their arrival is now as tall as the cottage.

We are so fortunate.

Zephaniah Smith arrived in town seeking revenge. Instead, he found redemption. *And he helped us start a new life of our own.*

Henry turns in the saddle to look beyond the cottage. On the land once claimed by Chadwick, a Māori family is tending a large vegetable garden bordered by stones. One of them looks up and waves. Henry returns the wave, then dismounts.

He calls out to the boy in the window: "Little Zed! Kia ora!"

"Papa!" The boy runs out, carrying his toy rifle. Henry puts the gun aside and sweeps the boy into his arms.

Miriama appears at the door in gardening clothes and waves.

Henry's mother joins her, and she and Miriama watch as he lifts his son in the air.

"Come inside, Little Zed, and I'll tell you a story," he says. "It's about bad men… and guns."

"Yay!" the boy cries out.

Doctor Henry smiles at his mother and his wife, and tells his son, "Your mama and grand-mama are in the story too. And a man called Zephaniah – just like you."

Henry reaches into the doctor's bag and pulls out Johnny Slick's dime novel.

The boy studies the cover and sounds out the words: "Henry Appleton – boy hero!"

He looks up at his father. "Is it a true story, Papa?"

Doc Henry smiles. "It is mostly true, Little Zed. Mostly true."

———

Later that year, Dr Henry Appleton, his wife Miriama Te Aroha Appleton and their son Zephaniah William Appleton sail to England, where they meet Queen Victoria.

Henry spends days searching for his birth mother, without success.

They travel home via America and visit the writer Johnny Slick. He takes them to meet President Ulysses Grant.

They arrive back in New Zealand in 1878. Miriama becomes a teacher, and Henry serves the Nelson community as a physician for the rest of his days.

THE END

A CRIME THAT SHOCKED THE COUNTRY

The Physician's Gun is a work of fiction, but it was inspired by a true event: the Maungatapu Murders, carried out by the ruthless Burgess gang. Descriptions of their evil deeds can be found in numerous books and newspaper articles. (See 'References and Further Reading' later in this book.)

A detailed account can be found on the New Zealand History website, but here is a summary:

On 12 June 1866, James Battle was murdered on the Maungatapu track, south-east of Nelson. The following day four other men were killed nearby – a crime that shocked the colony. These killings, the work of the 'Burgess gang', resembled something from the American 'wild west'.

The case was made more intriguing by the fact that one of the gang, Joseph Sullivan, turned on his co-accused and provided the evidence that convicted them. The trial was followed with great interest, and sketches and accounts of the case were eagerly snapped up by the public. Unlike his colleagues, Sullivan escaped the gallows.

An early composite of the so-called Maungatapu
Murderers: Philip Levy (top), Richard Burgess (left),
Thomas Kelly (right) and Joseph Sullivan (bottom).
(*Maungatapu Murderers*. Nelson Provincial
Museum Collection: 319996)

All four members of the Burgess gang had come to New
Zealand via the goldfields of Victoria, Australia. Three of
them had been transported to Australia for crimes
committed in England. They were the sort of 'career criminals' that the authorities in Otago had feared would arrive
following the discovery of gold in the province.

The gang's ringleader, originally known as Richard Hill,

had been transported from London to Melbourne for theft at the age of sixteen. After his release he resumed a life of crime and served several prison terms. By 1861 he was calling himself Burgess, the name of a New South Wales runholder he had attempted to rob. In January 1862 he left Australia for the Otago goldfields, where he teamed up with Thomas Noon, an acquaintance from his prison days in Australia. They specialised in attacking and robbing lone prospectors.

In March 1862, members of the Otago Mounted Police tried to bring Burgess and Noon in for questioning over a robbery on the Otago goldfields. Gunfire broke out and the pair fled, but were eventually captured. They were sentenced to 3½ years' hard labour in Dunedin Jail. After receiving thirty-six lashes for his role in another escape bid, Burgess vowed to exact revenge on society by taking a life for every lash.

On their release, Burgess and Noon (now calling himself Thomas Kelly) headed for the West Coast goldfields and staked a claim inland from Hokitika. Just before Christmas they carried out a series of robberies. Burgess was now living with a woman named Carrie who was pregnant with his child. His plan was to rob the bank at Ōkārito, south of Hokitika, and move back to Australia with her.

In the meantime, William (alias Philip) Levy arrived in Hokitika. He had emigrated to Victoria in the 1850s and established himself as a gold buyer. He also worked as a 'fence' (a seller of stolen goods) and passed on information about possible targets for robbery. In Hokitika he helped Burgess and Kelly plan robberies.

In April 1866 the gang was completed by another recent arrival from Victoria. Joseph Sullivan had been transported from England in 1840 for robbery, but by 1853 had established himself as a prize-fighter and publican.

On 28 May the gang murdered George Dobson, a surveyor whom they mistook for a gold buyer. Undeterred, they set up an ambush of the real gold buyer, but they were thwarted by the police and given 48 hours to leave town.

Using assumed names, Burgess, Sullivan and Kelly joined Levy aboard the *Wallaby* and departed for Westport with plans to rob the bank there. Finding that it had closed, they continued on to Nelson.

They arrived in Nelson nearly penniless on 6 June, and considered robbing one of the town's three banks, but found the police presence too great. Instead, they decided to walk the 70 miles to Picton and try their luck there. They travelled via the rugged Maungatapu Track, which would take them past the Wakamarina goldfield.

On 10 June they arrived at the goldfields settlement of Canvas Town, 40 miles short of Picton. Levy set about finding a possible target for the gang. At nearby Deep Creek, he met Felix Mathieu, a publican and storekeeper. He and three associates, James Dudley, John Kempthorne and James de Pontius, were about to leave for the West Coast, carrying money and gold. When Levy informed the others, plans were made to ambush the travellers near the summit of the Maungatapu Track.

The gang left Canvas Town early on 12 June and were passed on the track by James Battle. Burgess and Sullivan, concerned about potential witnesses, throttled him and buried him in a shallow grave.

They attacked the Mathieu party on 13 June, killing them one by one. Dudley was strangled, Kempthorne and de Pontius were shot, and Mathieu was both shot and stabbed. The gang acquired cash and gold dust worth £320 (nearly $35,000 in today's money).

The gang continued on to Nelson, where they booked into different hotels under false names. Next day they sold the gold and divided the proceeds equally before deciding to lie low for seven days, then travel to New Plymouth by ship.

Unbeknown to the gang, a friend of Mathieu's suspected foul play when they failed to arrive in Nelson. He reported their disappearance to police, and when a search party found some evidence of a crime, Levy was arrested. On 19 June his three associates were located and arrested too.

Without bodies, the police case was circumstantial. The government promised £200 (more than $21,000) and a free pardon to any accomplice (not the actual murderer) who turned Queen's evidence, and Sullivan took the offer. He claimed to have been merely a lookout for the gang, and told the police about the killing of James Battle and incriminated the others. The bodies of Mathieu, Dudley, Kempthorne and de Pontius were recovered thanks to Sullivan's evidence. Battle's body was found three days later.

Awaiting trial, Burgess wrote a long statement – 'The Confessions of Burgess the Murderer' – in which he detailed his many crimes and exonerated Kelly and Levy.

The case went to the Supreme Court. A special sitting opened in Nelson on 12 September with Mr Justice Johnston of Wellington as trial judge.

In accordance with the terms of the amnesty, Sullivan was not charged. Burgess, conducting his own defence, was determined to implicate Sullivan directly in the killings and cross-examined him for 15 hours without success.

The judge spent more than six hours summing up the case for the jury. He described Burgess as an 'arch plotter', a 'cruel assassin' and 'one of the wickedest of men'. The jury took less than an hour to find all three men guilty of murder. Kelly collapsed and was taken away sobbing, while Levy continued to maintain his innocence.

Members of the Nelson Volunteers surrounded the jail on the morning of the execution to ensure that 'good order was maintained'. Before bounding up the scaffold steps, Burgess declared that 'he had no more fear of death than he had of going to a wedding'. He selected the central noose and kissed it as 'a prelude to heaven'. Kelly had to be carried up, while Levy calmly protested his innocence. There was a delay while the three condemned men made their final statements. Kelly was still speaking when – just before 8.30am – the hangman drew the bolt that opened the trapdoor.

Moulds for casts of the three heads were taken as a contribution to phrenology, a then-popular discipline that would eventually be dismissed as pseudo-science. Adherents of phrenology claimed that personal characteristics could be determined from the shape of an individual's head.

The bodies were buried in the prison yard.

The full story:

https://nzhistory.govt.nz/culture/further-sources-maungatapu-murders

HISTORICAL PHOTOGRAPHS

Some extraordinary photographs from the 1860s – including portraits of the Burgess gang – can be found in the archives of our public libraries. A selection of these appear on the following pages. Studying old photos can provide useful information about the buildings, streets, clothes and hairstyles of the 1860s.

The author of *The Physician's Gun*, John Evan Harris, inspecting the so-called 'death masks' of the three hanged highwaymen at the Nelson Provincial Museum. From left: Richard Burgess, Thomas Kelly and Philip Levy.

The Nelson Provincial Museum has a wonderful online collection, especially the Tyree Studio Collection. (Although many of these photos were taken in the 1870s, later than the 1866 setting of *The Physician's Gun*, we can assume that clothing and street scenes did not change too much in those few years.) The museum also has 3800 negatives taken by William Davis during his time in Nelson.

Richard Burgess

This is the only known image of Richard Burgess: a photo taken shortly after his arrest. He was charismatic, manipulative and complex. The writer Mark Twain remarked that Burgess's 'confession' was "a remarkable paper... perhaps without its peer in the literature of murder."

Born Richard Hill in 1829 in London, it's believed Burgess was the illegitimate son of a ladies' maid and possibly a member of the Horse Guards. His mother fell on hard times and young Richard became a pickpocket and then a housebreaker. He was jailed and then shipped off to Melbourne. He became a proficient stonemason but returned to a life of crime, and in 1852 was sentenced to 10 years for a robbery which he proclaimed he did not commit. He endured years of harsh punishment in Melbourne prisons and the notorious floating prison hulks. Hill changed his name to Burgess and came to New Zealand in 1862 where he was soon involved in violent robberies on the Otago goldfield. (*Richard Burgess*. Nelson Provincial Museum Collection: C1849)

Joseph Thomas Sullivan

A photograph of Joseph Thomas Sullivan taken shortly after his arrest. Born in Ireland to Catholic parents, schooled in London, a boxer and baker, he was convicted of burglary aged around twenty-five and sent to Australia. He married and had two sons, and ran a public house for a decade in

Victoria before coming to New Zealand in 1866. Sometimes referred to as 'Flash Tom', he managed to wriggle his way out of being put on trial with Burgess and the other gang members, but was promptly tried and found guilty of the murder of the flax-cutter James Battle. After serving a prison sentence in New Zealand he returned to Australia. He was widely loathed by the public not only because they thought he had been an active member of the Burgess gang but also because they believed he took part in the murder of the young surveyor George Dobson – for which he was never tried. (*Mr Joseph Thomas Sullivan. Maungatapu Murderers' Gang*. Nelson Provincial Museum Collection: 318174)

Thomas Kelly

A photograph of Thomas Kelly, taken shortly after his arrest. He was born Thomas Noon in London in 1825, to poor but respectable Catholic parents. After committing many petty thefts and burglary he was transported to

Australia. He again took up a life of crime, which continued when he went to New Zealand and teamed up with Richard Burgess. (*Thomas Kelly*. Nelson Provincial Museum Collection: C1848).

William Philip Levy

William Philip Levy was photographed along with the other members of the gang, shortly after their arrest. Born in London in 1831 to Jewish parents, Levy immigrated to Victoria as a free immigrant – unlike his fellow gang members. But although he set up as a general trader in the Otago goldfields he was suspected of being a 'fence' – selling stolen goods – and of helping criminals to identify potential targets for robbery. He was recruited by Burgess to do just that, and soon became an active member of the gang – although he went to the gallows professing his innocence. (*Mr William Levy, Maungatapu Murderers gang*. Nelson Provincial Museum Collection: 318110.)

When four businessmen went missing on Maungatapu Mountain, foul play was suspected. This poster was printed, and Joseph Sullivan, already under suspicion and languishing in prison, saw the offer of a free pardon for an accomplice and jumped at it. He became Queen's Evidence and insisted at the trial of his accomplices that he did not take part in any actual murders. (Marlborough Museum, Marlborough Historical Society Collection 1994.040.0005)

Sergeant John Nash

Perhaps he does not look like the heroic law enforcement officer that Henry Appleton perceived him to be, but Sergeant John Nash was certainly a dedicated lawman. According to the NZ Police website, John Nash was born in Killarney, Ireland, about 1822. He sailed for New Zealand in 1845 with the 65th Regiment of the British Army. On leaving the Army in 1857 he joined the Nelson Provincial Armed Constabulary as a constable and was promoted to Sergeant in 1863. He was third in command of the

Provincial Police Force in Nelson, and for his work in the hunt for the Burgess gang he was awarded a gold watch. Nash was registered as the first non-commissioned member of the newly formed New Zealand Police Force on 1 September, 1886. He had the number '1' displayed prominently on his headgear. (Sergeant John Nash, July 1887. Nelson Provincial Museum, W E Brown Collection: 16898)

Gustavus Ferdinand von Tempsky

Gustavus Ferdinand von Tempsky became a folk hero in his brief but spectacular military career in New Zealand. He was born into a Prussian family with a long military tradition. After a brief time with the Royal Prussian Army, then digging unsuccessfully for gold in California and Australia, he sailed to New Zealand with his wife and young family in 1862.

On the Coromandel Peninsula he was a gold miner and newspaper correspondent but on the outbreak of war in 1863 he joined the Forest Rangers. They were an 'irregular' force intended to match the Māori who were skilled at fighting in the bush. As leader of his own company, he had large steel Bowie knives made for his men, and they used the short-barrelled Calisher and Terry .54 carbine, which was ideal for close quarter fighting. Von Tempsky himself carried two Colt Navy .36 pistols and was often pictured with a sabre which he carried unsheathed when expecting battle. Called "Von" by some of his men, he emerged as a very effective leader who inspired great loyalty. He was known to the Māori as Manurau, "the bird that flits everywhere". The flamboyant and handsome Von Tempsky was also a talented amateur artist and singer.

But he was a self-publicist, described as being 'avid for glory and admiration,' and his impetuous nature led to his downfall. During a misguided and premature attack on Tītokowaru's main fighting pā, he took one too many risks and was killed by a bullet through his forehead. He died aged only 40. (Gustavus Ferdinand von Tempsky. Making New Zealand: Negatives and prints from the Making New Zealand Centennial collection. Ref: MNZ-

0876-1/4-F. Alexander Turnbull Library, Wellington, New Zealand https://natlib.govt.nz/records/22308963.)

Charles Canning. Nelson Provincial Museum, Tyree Studio Collection: 67863.

This is Charles Canning, a prominent Nelson farmer and businessman who was foreman of the special jury at the trial of the Maungatapu murderers. He was a benefactor who donated or sold land for various community activities, at one stage held the important role of Chief Inspector of Sheep, and was well known for planting a large number of trees in the district. He married Catherine Jane McRae in 1862 and they had two children – Elizabeth Sarah and William Davis. Because his son was ill he took his family back to England in 1884, and he died in Somerset in 1892 at the age of 64.

Trafalgar Street, circa 1863. Nelson Provincial Museum, Kingsford Collection: half 743.

This photograph gives us a good idea of what Nelson looked like when Richard Burgess and his gang came to town after their murderous exploits on Maungatapu Mountain. The photo was taken in 1863, just three years before the murders, looking south up Trafalgar Street to Church Hill and the Cathedral. To the left of the cathedral are several buildings, possibly including the Court House and jail.

Nelson foothills, 1860s. Nelson Provincial Museum, Kingsford Collection: 156001.

This photograph, taken in the Nelson foothills in Burgess's time, shows the area was still sparsely-occupied by settlers. But the European influences are plain to see in the design of houses and fences, and the rather unsuitable clothing they insisted on wearing. (Note the long dresses of the two women at the lower end of the fence line!) Perhaps the most remarkable feature of the scene is the lack of native bush and forest: most of the majestic trees have already been felled for timber for houses and other buildings, and for ships' masts, railway sleepers, fence posts, furniture and export. And firewood.

Trafalgar Hotel. Nelson Provincial Museum, Tyree
Studio Collection: 34911.

The Trafalgar Hotel, one of many in the district, stood prominently at the corner of Trafalgar and Bridge Streets.

West's Shop. Nelson Provincial Museum, Davis
Collection: 10279

W.H. West's Saloon and Tobacconist in Hardy Street,

where many of Nelson's menfolk would go for a haircut and shave, to read the newspapers, and to chat. The shop sold toys, fireworks, gun powder and shot for firearms. It also offered hot and cold baths.

REFERENCES AND FURTHER READING

Suggestions from John Evan Harris, author of The Physician's Gun

EARLY NEWSPAPERS AND OTHER ONLINE RESOURCES

If reading *The Physician's Gun* has encouraged you to find out more about Colonial New Zealand, I recommend you look up the early newspapers. Many of them are available online, and make for great reading:

Nelson newspapers – the *Nelson Examiner, The Colonist, Nelson Evening Mail* – sourced from the National Library. (www.paperspast.natlib.govt.nz).

The Early New Zealand Books Collection (http://www.enzb.auckland.ac.nz/docs/2014AucklandMuseum/1867-stevens-and-b/pdf/1867-stevens-and-b1003.pdf) is a treasure trove developed by staff at the University of Auckland Libraries and Learning Services. It includes an enormous amount of detail on the Burgess Gang trials, including:

- **'The Confession of Burgess, The Murderer'**, Burgess's own account of his life and the Maungatapu Murders, written in his cell as he awaited trial.

- **'Illustrated narrative of the dreadful murders on the Maungatapu Mountain'**. A 'pamphlet' compiled in 1866 by Nelson Colonist editor David M. Luckie, it promises reports on *'Five men foully murdered by bushrangers. Capture of the four murderers. Trial, conviction, & execution.'* This publication certainly delivers, in huge detail.

- **Nelson Colonist reports** on the trial, in great detail, from the opening day through to the judge passing the sentence of death on the three men, and the subsequent hangings. It also covers
- 'The Trial of Sullivan for the murder of Battle'.

Stevens and Bartholomew's New Zealand directory for 1866-67, available from the National Library (https://natlib.govt.nz/records/20602794) and the Early NZ Books collection (http://www.enzb.auckland.ac.nz/docs/2014Auckland   Museum/1867-stevens-and-b/pdf) among many other libraries, contains a list of inhabitants of Nelson and their occupations. A wonderful insight into the makeup of Nelson's community in the days of *The Physician's Gun.*

The Prow (http://www.theprow.org.nz), a website featuring historical and cultural stories from Nelson, Tasman and Marlborough, is a wonderful resource for researchers and teachers. It's a collaboration between the Nelson City, Tasman and Marlborough District Libraries, Nelson Marlborough Institute of Technology and The Nelson Provincial Museum, and among its treasures are the digitized journals of the Nelson Historical Society.

REFERENCE BOOKS

There are many books available in your library – a few of which I have read, and acknowledge:

'The Nelson Police – The story of the Nelson Police District 1841–1986' by June E. Neale.

'Te Tau Ihu o Te Waka: A history of Māori of Nelson and Marlborough, **Volume II: Te Ara Hou – The New Society'** by Hilary and John Mitchell (Huia Publishers in association with Wakatū Incorporation.) This is an exhaustively researched and referenced book with first-hand accounts by early European settlers, and many illustrations.

- The conflict between traditional Māori beliefs and Christianity: Page 124
- A European visitor's description of a pā and the Māori way of life: Page 155
- A description of urupā (burial sites) including pictures of upright monuments: Page 439–442

'**Nelson – A history of early settlement**' by Ruth M. Allan (A H & A W Reed 1965), available through the Nelson Provincial Museum. This impressively-detailed book mainly concerns the 1839 – 1844 period, although some parts go up to the 1850s. It has a great deal of well-researched facts about the New Zealand Company, NZ-UK politics, the governors/company agents, land dealings. Also: The Wairau Incident/Massacre/Affray of 1843.

'**Murder on the Maungatapu**' by Wayne Martin (Canterbury University Press, 2016).

'**Confessions of Richard Burgess**' by David Burton (AH & AW Reed, 1983).

'**In Deadly Earnest**': A collection of fiction by New Zealand Women 1870s – 1980s, introduced and collected by Trudie McNaughton. (Century Hutchinson Ltd, 1989.)

'**The Penguin History of New Zealand**' by Michael King (Penguin Books NZ Ltd, 2003).

'**Diggers Hatters & Whores**': The story of the NZ Gold Rushes by Stevan Eldred-Grigg (Random House New Zealand, 2008)

A Legal History of the New Zealand Jury Service – Introduction, Evolution and Equality?" [1999] VUWLawRw 19; (1999) 29(2) by Michele Powles (Victoria University of Wellington Law Review 283).

'**Old New Zealand Houses 1800 – 1940**' by Jeremy Salmond (Reed Books.)

'**Working away, unseen: stories of the lives of Nelson women**' by STEM Writers of Nelson (STEM Writers, 2019)

'**Labour, Faith & Favour**' by Mary Ellen O'Connor (Mary Ellen O'Connor, 2018).

Journal of the Nelson and Marlborough Historical Societies (Victoria University), Volume 2, issue 1, 1987.

'**How is the river? A Takaka Valley History**' by Jane McDonald (River Press, 2017).

'**Colonial Experiences in New Zealand**' by 'An Old Colonist', believed to be William Pratt. (Chapman Hall, 1877.)

'**Exotic Intruders**' by Joan Druett (Heinemann, 1983), part of the Victoria University of Wellington Library's online New Zealand Texts Collection: a description of the trees and plants encountered by early European settlers.

'**Birdstories: a history of the birds of New Zealand**', by Geoff Norman (Potton and Burton, Nelson 2018.) A wonderfully illustrated book where it's fun to learn the Māori words for Aotearoa's huge range of birds: the kākāriki, pīwakawaka, tūi, kererū, korimako, pītoitoi, kōtare, kakaruwai, piopio, pīpīwharauroa, pīhoihoi, tītitipounamu, pīwauwau, pihipihi, hihi, riroriro...

'**Ngā Waka Māori: Māori Canoes**' by Anne Nelson (Macmillan Co of New Zealand, 1991).

'**The Victorian Hospital**' by Lavinia Mitton (Shire Publications Ltd, 2001).

'**Life in Victorian Britain**' by Michael St John Parker (Pitkin Publishing, Pavilion Books Company, 1999).

'**Handguns and Police in New Zealand 1840 – 1990**' by John Osborne (South Pacific Armoury, 1990).

THE WORLD OF JOHNNY SLICK

If you're interested in the world inhabited by the American dime novel author Johnny Slick, you may be able to obtain a rare copy of his novel '**Henry Appleton, Boy Hero, and the Burgess Gang.**' You might research the writers of other early dime novels, or the outlaws who featured in their wildly-popular books.

'**Dime Novel Desperadoes: the notorious Maxwell Brothers**', by John E Hallwas (University of Illinois Press 2011).

You might like to read one of the many books written by Ned Buntline (real name Colonel E. Z. C. Judson), the American writer who inspired the character of Johnny Slick:

'**Buffalo Bill and his adventures in the West**' by Ned Buntline (J. S.

Ogilvie and Company, New York 1886), reprinted in 2006 by Stonecrest Industries (www.stonecrestindustries.com).

'Wild Bill's Last Trail' by Ned Buntline (Dodo Press).

WORTH A VISIT

The Nelson Provincial Museum (www.nelsonmuseum.co.nz) is in the centre of town at the corner of Trafalgar and Hardy Streets. It contains a wealth of exhibits from early Nelson – and specifically, a section on the Burgess Gang. Here you can see the plaster cast 'death masks' of the three hanged men, featured in *The Physician's Gun*, plus fascinating items such as Burgess's crucifix-shaped document.

Nelson Cathedral (www.nelsoncathedral.org) is a magnificent building which sits on the hill known as Pikimai, which translates as 'climb hither'. The hill has a commanding view of the town and the NZ Company quickly set up camp here. After the Wairau incident in which several prominent Nelson leaders died, fearful townsfolk built a redoubt here and named it Fort Arthur. Later there was parish church here (built in 1851) which Richard Burgess and his gang couldn't have failed to see, as it dominated the main street, although they probably didn't visit it. The cathedral wasn't built until more than 60 years after the Burgess gang terrified the town, but there are many reminders of turbulent earlier times including a wall plaque which reads simply "In Memory of those who fell at the Wairau, 17th of June 1843."

Isel House (nelson.govt.nz/iselhouse), off the main road, Stoke, was constructed by the Marsden family in the 1840s and onwards, using local stone. It contains old furniture and paintings and is surrounded by a woodland of heritage trees.

Broadgreen Historic House (nelson.govt.nz/broadgreen) is at 276 Nayland Road, Stoke. Built in 1855, it contains a collection of garments and everyday items, and boasts a magnificent garden which includes roses and other flowers and trees planted by early European settlers.

Founders Heritage Park (www.founderspark.co.nz) at 87 Atawhai Drive contains well-maintained houses, church and workshops and offices of the time including a replica of the Nelson Evening Mail newspaper office. The restored Duncan House has information and pictures relating to the ill-fated New Zealand Company. There are sketches of notable Māori and European men and women of the 1800s plus information on Edward Gibbon Wakefield and his Nelson Settlement dream.

Wakapuaka cemetery is a picturesque and well-maintained historic site which contains the graves of many early settlers plus the monument to the memory of the victims of the Burgess gang. (http://www.nelson.-govt.nz/services/facilities/cemeteries/cemeteries-in-nelson-2/waka-puaka-cemetery)

The South Street Heritage Precinct off Nile Street, is New Zealand's oldest fully-preserved street, where you can see modest but well-preserved cottages built for renting to local tradesmen in the 1860s.

THE AUTHOR, JOHN EVAN HARRIS

As a television producer and founder of Greenstone Pictures, John Evan Harris was able to indulge his passion for true stories with series like the award-winning re-enactment show *Epitaph*. Originated by actor Paul Gittins, *Epitaph* told the stories of people who met untimely or dramatic deaths. John: "We dramatized the fascinating life and death events of real people."

It was an *Epitaph* episode, based on the 1866 Maungatapu Murders, which inspired him to write *The Physician's Gun*.

John was born in Christchurch, and spent a few years in Nelson as a child, but has lived most of his life in Auckland. He worked as a reporter for newspapers, radio and TV, served as programme editor of TVNZ's regional news magazine show *Top Half*, and joined Communicado to produce shows like *Heroes* and *That's Fairly Interesting*.

In 1994 he set up production company Greenstone Pictures, which produced dozens of documentaries and factual series which sold around the world. He sold Greenstone in 2014 to set up Boy Fell In Pond and become a full-time writer.

Movies are his first love, and he is happy to focus on writing film scripts. "My dream is to make small movies with a big heart which sell internationally."

John's three siblings have all written books, but *The Physician's Gun* is John's first.

The author lived in Nelson as a child, and recalls feeding the ducks in the famous Queen's Gardens. The pool was known by Māori as the Eel Pond and eels still survive in the pond today. But in 1887 the area was renamed in honour of the 50th Jubilee of the coronation of Queen Victoria, and eventually transformed into a heritage Victorian public garden extending between Hardy and Bridge Streets.

John's author website: www.johnevanharris.com
His company: www.boyfellinpond.com

THE COVER ARTIST, MINKY STAPLETON

Award-winning artist Minky Stapleton designed the cover for *The Physician's Gun*.

Minky, who is based in Auckland, has had exhibitions in South Africa and Australia, designed costumes for a rock opera, created book covers for best-selling authors, illustrated picture books, designed a T-shirt for Hilary Clinton, "and done a whole lot of other stuff in between". More recently she has been illustrating children's books and has finally written her own book dedicated to her crazy dog, Scooby. Keep an eye out for *Roo and Vladimir* (published by Scholastic) at your local bookstore.

THE ILLUSTRATOR, CHARLES CUMMING

Charles Cumming (left) and the author at their first meeting to discuss illustrations for *The Physician's Gun*.

The illustrations inside *The Physician's Gun* were drawn by Auckland artist Charles Cumming.

Author John Evan Harris says: "Charles has done a great job of capturing the spirit of the book, using the style of line drawings of the day. His pictures make the book so much more interesting and accessible for young readers."

Charles works mainly in 3-D animation. "I've always loved art and did art classes at school," he says. "I was one of those kids that was constantly drawing. I never stopped. I ended up going to design school and currently work as a 3-D artist, making things in the computer that get rendered and placed into film and TV."

His assignment for *The Physician's Gun* is his first of this type. "Drawing has always been part of the design process, a way to quickly solve problems and brainstorm – but I've never done drawing as anything more than a hobby until this project.

"It's been great collaborating, and pushing myself outside of my comfort zone."

THE DIME NOVELIST, JOHNNY SLICK

Author of:

Henry Appleton – Boy Hero and the Burgess Gang
Shootout at Dead Man's Creek
Wild Bill and the Indian Outlaw
Masters of the Prairie
Gunfight on the High Plateau

Little is known about the American novelist Johnny Slick (real name Robert Robertson). He claimed to be – and probably was – a prolific writer. But it is very unlikely he penned more books than his contemporary Colonel E Z C Judson. Under the pseudonym Ned Buntline, Judson is reputed to have written some 300 dime novels, including *Buffalo Bill and his adventures in the West.*

Slick's novel, *'Henry Appleton – Boy Hero!'* is the only one which can reliably be attributed to Robertson, although Henry Appleton was in no doubt that Robertson was the author of *Shootout at Dead Man's Creek* and *Masters of the Prairie.*

The only photo of a man presumed to be novelist Johnny Slick.

It is possible Robertson was born around 1820 somewhere in Oklahoma, but the place and date of his death are

unknown. We know he was in New Zealand in 1866, because of his extensive writings about the Burgess Gang, and some believe he may have died here. But he was certainly back in the United States by 1875, when he published his novel *'Henry Appleton – Boy Hero!'*

Robertson led a colourful life, punctuated by frequent brushes with the law, and if he is to be believed he was often in the company of some of America's most famous sons. As he told Henry Appleton, he once challenged the outlaw Wild Bill Hickok to a duel which ended in farce because both men were too drunk to aim effectively.

There is one unverified report that a gravestone, possibly that of Robert Robertson, was uncovered in New Zealand in the early 1900s. Its inscription read *'Here lies the famed American author Robert Robertson, also known as Johnny Slick, who died heroically rescuing a young mother and her children from the raging Waikato River.'* It is possible this report is just a story, as unreliable as any of Johnny Slick's adventures, and even if it were true is it likely the inscription was drafted by the dime novelist himself.

This writer would welcome more information about Robert Robertson and his alter ego Johnny Slick. Sometimes one wonders if he ever existed.

John Harris, author of *'The Physician's Gun'*.

ACKNOWLEDGMENTS

Through the best part of a decade, in between other projects, I have received enormous encouragement from family and friends. I first wrote the story as a film script (which I hope will one day make it to the big screen), and in 2020 decided to put my research to good use in the form of this book.

I offer heartfelt thanks to my family Sarah, Matthew, Mandy and Emily who encouraged and questioned, offered ideas and in the case of Mandy and Emily provided huge amounts of research on New Zealand in the 1860s; my late wife Noelene who endured long hours of silence as I scoured through books and old newspaper articles and built the 'world' of Henry Appleton and Zephaniah Smith; my siblings Peter, Rose and Penny who encouraged me and offered challenging feedback; my wife Jan Zane Harris who brainstormed, edited, encouraged and corrected; my personal trainer/guru Mike Ansari who immersed himself in the story and offered ideas for the title of the book – including my final choice – and self-publishing expert Martin Taylor who came aboard in the final phase to make this book a reality.

I am indebted to Nelson-based researchers Hilary and John Mitchell, authors of the awesomely detailed '*Te Tau Ihu o Te Waka: A history of Māori of Nelson and Marlborough*' who generously gave me their time to listen to my story and gently put me on the right track.

I thank the staff at the Nelson Provincial Museum, Nelson Public Libraries and Founders Heritage Park, whose work in preserving the history of Nelson has provided material and background for *The Physician's Gun*.

And I am deeply grateful for the expertise of antique gun authority John Milligan, who provided me with technical and practical advice on the weapons described in this story.

John Evan Harris